Jane Lark

I love writing authentic, passionate and emotional love stories. I began my first novel, a historical, when I was sixteen, but life derailed me a bit when I started suffering with Ankylosing Spondylitis, so I didn't complete a novel until after I was thirty when I put it on my to do before I'm forty list. Now I love getting caught up in the lives and traumas of my characters, and I'm so thrilled to be giving my characters life in others' imaginations, especially when readers tell me they've read the characters just as I've tried to portray them.

www.janelark.co.uk

@JaneLark

PRAISE FOR JANE LARK

I'm Keeping You

JANE LARK

A division of HarperCollins*Publishers*
www.harpercollins.co.uk

Harper*Impulse* an imprint of
HarperCollins*Publishers*
1 London Bridge Street
London SE1 9GF

www.harpercollins.co.uk

A Paperback Original 2016

First published in Great Britain in ebook format by Harper*Impulse* 2016

A catalogue record for this book
is available from the British Library

ISBN: 9780008139896

Set in Minion by Palimpsest Book Production Ltd, Falkirk, Stirlingshire

Printed and bound in Great Britain

MIX
Paper from
responsible sources
FSC® C007454

Thank you to my wonderful editor, Charlotte Ledger, who has worked with me for the last two years, for believing in my work, seeing the potential in Jason and putting a romance book out about a good guy, which turned into the *Starting Out* series full of good guys. Thank you, Charlotte, for giving me the freedom to write the stories I want to tell and helping me to make them stronger.

Also I'm sure you'll all want to join me in thanking the cover artists, Alexandra Allden and Zoe Jackson, for giving you some wonderful images to look at as you read the stories.

Then there's one more thank you, to you all, for reading the series, and taking the time to share and post reviews and message me on Facebook and through Twitter, to tell me how much you love the books. I love hearing from you, and it's great to know that people really understand and enjoy getting caught up in the stories and characters. Thank you.

CHAPTER ONE

Rachel

I drifted from sleep to dreams to being half awake. The things Jason and I had talked about at the party the other night were stopping me from sleeping, plus the conversation we'd had with our solicitor.

Thoughts swept through my head, about my ex, Declan, and New York and meeting the guy I'd been meant to find—Jason.

I rolled on to my back. My forearm lifted to my forehead as an image of Saint came into my mind. I slid back into sleep.

I picked him up out of his buggy. My beautiful son.

We were standing on a bridge, looking at the river in the park. I showed him the clear water as we leaned over the railing. "Look, you can see the fish." I could see them. The water wasn't like the Hudson. It was a narrow, shallow river. I could see right to the bottom. The weeds waved, making patterns in the flow of the current as the water headed on out to join a bigger river and make its way to the coast.

The heat of the sun warmed the skin on my face and my arms. I felt superhuman, like I had a super-power. I was the best mom in the world. I was high, full of energy and charged up. Ideas fizzed around in my head. We were going to go back and paint, and bake.

A play-dough recipe—I should Google a play-dough recipe.

"Maybe I should ask Grampy to build you a sandpit. You need

a sandpit, don't you, Saint…" I looked down at the fish. Their tails swished at the water as they swam against the current.

"And you need a fishing rod, to go fishing, and a little net. But I guess a net first. Maybe we should go get a net now, so we can catch a fish."

I lifted Saint up high, holding him above my head, above the railing. Not Lion-King style but so he looked down at me as I looked up at him. The sun shone behind him, giving my little Saint a halo. He made his three-month-old gurgling sound.

I felt like Mufasa, though, or perhaps more like Sarabi; like I was the *queen* lioness. I'd only just discovered Disney. Disney movies were one of the new exciting mommy things in my life. My mom had never done being a mom. I'd never stepped inside a cinema when I was a kid, or watched a movie on TV.

Since Saint was born, I'd sat down and watched more than a dozen movies with him, loads of times. I was different from Mom. I was a good mom. The best. And Saint was going to be the President, because I was going to bring him up so well, and he'd stand up before Congress and tell everyone he owed it all to his amazing mommy.

I brought him down and hugged him tight. I loved hugging him the most. Squeezing my little, solid, happy human being. My body had made him; this perfect little boy.

Sunshine heated my hair and face. I looked down at the water. It looked so cool. Jason used to swim here when he'd been a kid. He'd told me. It looked refreshing. I'd never swum in a river. I could have hardly gone for a dip in the Hudson back in New York, or dived into the Delaware when I'd lived in Philadelphia as a kid. But here, this was only a little, narrow river. "Saint, you oughta learn to swim. I bet you'd love it. Daddy said it was always fun… He liked it."

I held Saint against my chest and walked off the bridge, leaving his buggy behind. "I bet the water's refreshing. It'll be nice on a hot day like this."

There was an area where the bank sloped down toward the water. It was flat by the water's edge.

I walked down there. "We're gonna swim, Saint."

I walked to the edge and kept walking, the cool water washing over my sneakers. It was a lovely sensation. I could see me teaching Saint to swim, holding his hands as he kicked out. I'd seen babies swimming in ads. Saint could do that. He was a clever baby. The water came up to my knees, getting the hem of my skirt wet, but I didn't stop walking. I loved the cool sensation pushing against my legs and caressing my skin as the water ran around me and flowed on downstream. It was exciting to be in a river—to do what Jason had done as a kid. I was the best mom.

The water came up to my waist and surged against me, swirling around me, creating little eddies. Saint's toes dipped into the river, they were bare, it was a warm day; I hadn't put socks on his feet. He made a gurgling sound.

"Does the water tickle?"

My clothes were soaked and clinging to my body, but even that was nice—a good feeling—because they were cool—*and I was manically happy.*

The water spun in whirlpools just in front of us. It was dancing. The sunlight caught on the surface, making it sparkle. The world was magic. I imagined us swimming with the fish. I knew the whirlpools implied the current was stronger, but I was supermom—so that didn't matter to me. My mind was full of images of me teaching Saint to swim; there was no space in my head for other thoughts. I took another step out. The water was up to my shoulders and up to his shoulders, and it was so good. The current and the pressure of the flowing water pulled at my feet. I fought to keep my balance, but it didn't disturb me. Saint was just looking at me, with wide eyes, bemused by the new sensations. I laughed. I was going to let him go—I was going to let him swim.

"Hey! Hey! What the fuck are you doing?" A strange guy called out from the bank. He was yelling at me.

3

"Hey! You! Get back! You'll drown the kid!"

I hugged Saint tight as the guy waded into the water. He was trying to steal Saint. Another guy ran in and between them they got a hold of me and dragged me out. I fought against them, hanging on to Saint. But then the second guy growled into my ear. "What are you trying to do, kill him?"

The words punched me. *Kill him…* No. "No. I'm teaching him to swim!"

"He's a baby!"

One of the guys took Saint from my arms and began looking at him, all over, like he might be hurt. I sat on the bank shivering. The guys fussed over Saint, and they wouldn't give him back. Other people came.

The water hadn't been cool, it had been cold. But I was just teaching Saint to swim.

"Hi. Yeah. Cops."

One of the guys had his cell to his ear.

"Yeah, some woman in the park just tried to drown her kid."

I stood up. "I didn't. I was teaching him to swim. Kids need to swim. His daddy used to swim here. We were just swimming." I hit the guy's arm and tried to take his cell.

"You weren't teaching him to swim…" the guy who held Saint growled at me.

I held out my hands. I wanted to go home now. "Let me have him."

The guy held on to him.

"Let me have him!" Panic pulled tight around my chest, solidifying in my lungs, as euphoria spun into fear. The guy's face became Declan's face.

"Let me have him!"

The guy wouldn't let me take him back. My baby. "He's mine! Let me have him! He's mine!" My screams became louder and louder.

4

"Hey. You okay?" Jason's hand ran over my shoulder. When I opened my eyes, I escaped the dream, but every muscle in my body trembled from the shock and fear. It hadn't been a dream. I'd walked into that river for real with my three-month-old baby, and it had changed our lives, maybe forever.

"You alright? You were dreaming..." Jason's arm wrapped around my shoulders then pulled me against his chest. We were in bed. The room was dark.

My forehead pressed into his shoulder and I shook my head. I wasn't alright. The cops had picked me up but they hadn't arrested me, they'd taken me to Jason's parents and explained what had happened. His mom had looked at me with pity, and his dad with confusion, and then they'd called Jason. He'd been working in the store. He'd closed the store that day. It was the only time I'd ever known him close the store.

But I hadn't waited for Jason to come home. I hadn't needed him to tell me I was a failure. I knew I was a failure. My mood had crashed, hurtling down. I'd walked out of his parents' house. I hadn't wanted to face Jason, and I hadn't wanted to see Saint.

I'd failed.

I didn't see how I could be a mom anymore—or a wife.

Jason had found me in a park, on a swing, hours later, I'd been lost in despair, it had been agony, a heavy, dense pain—too intense for words. I'd been too ill to even talk.

He'd called for an ambulance. It had taken me to the hospital. The doctors there had started me on a heavy dose of mood-controlling meds.

I didn't remember much about my days in the hospital.

"What were you dreaming of?"

"The river," I breathed against his skin.

His other hand stroked over my hair.

It was my stupid, distorted bipolar view of the world that had given my ex, Declan, Saint's biological father, a chance to take Saint. He was saying I was unfit to care for Saint because I'd

5

walked into the river. But I didn't understand why Declan wanted Saint. He had kids already and he hardly had anything to do with them. He didn't like kids. He was a shitty dad.

"It's going to be okay," Jason said over my head.

Jason was a good dad, but that didn't seem to matter, and it wasn't okay, nothing was okay, and that's why we were flying out to New York tomorrow and I was leaving Saint. Because I was a bad mom. I'd failed him.

My arm slipped about Jason's waist and I held on to him. His fingers gripped my shoulder and he pressed a kiss on to the crown of my head.

He'd never judged me for my error, just loved me. He understood me. He'd taken time to learn about my illness since we'd gotten married last year and he'd said a hundred times he knew it hadn't been a choice, I'd just been sick.

The anxiety that had clasped at my lungs and sent my pulse soaring into a manic dance rhythm in the dream swept back in. Terror. I was terrified of losing Jason. As terrified as I was of losing Saint. Maybe because Jason was so special, and I'd done nothing to deserve a good guy, so how could he keep loving me? But he still did. He'd spent hours in the last few days reassuring me he did and that him leaving me would never happen.

I fell asleep again, holding him, and being held by him... I belonged with him... and Saint belonged with him.

When I woke sunlight shone into our room in Jason's parents' house.

Jason wasn't in bed, or in the room, but I could hear Saint in his crib. I got up, picked him up, and held him tight, breathing in the smell of his hair as his breath stirred the tiny, fine hairs on my neck. Love was a great, deep well and it filled me up. The room became a shimmering blur. I'd die if I lost him as much as I'd die if I lost Jason. I wouldn't want to be alive without either of them. Before I'd met Jason and had Saint, I didn't even know if I could love a child, especially a child of Declan's. But I didn't think of Saint as Declan's, he wasn't. Saint was Jason's son, in every way that mattered. Jason had been around for Saint and me right from the get go, from the moment I'd discovered I was pregnant, not just when Saint was born.

He was still here. I hoped he always would be. That's what I wanted.

I brushed Saint's hair back and kissed his head, wiped away my tears, then walked over to the door, turned the handle and went to find Jason.

Saint babbled away in his baby language. He'd laughed the other day. On Halloween. At the silly Halloween trick Jason had bought him. That had been the best sound I'd ever heard.

I heard Jason talking to his mom in the kitchen. I walked in there, wearing one of his old tees and just my panties, my legs bare. I hugged Saint against my chest. Jason turned around, a smile broke his lips apart immediately. I loved it when he smiled like that—he hardly ever smiled like that now.

"Hey, honey." He walked across the room to us, and his fingers stroked over Saint's head as he leaned over to kiss my lips. "You okay?"

I nodded.

But we both knew I wasn't.

I'd been terrified for ages that he didn't love me anymore, I'd gotten so lost. I didn't know how to be me anymore since I'd gone on to this last batch of meds. But the other day, over Halloween, we'd talked stuff out, and he'd gotten cross that I even doubted it. He did still love me—us. I'd been telling myself that as much as he had in the last few days, trying to convince my head what my heart knew.

When we'd talked stuff out, we'd kind of found each other again—that's what he'd said. But I hadn't found my old self and he'd admitted that he missed the me I'd been before I'd started on the strong meds. I missed that person too—desperately. She used to laugh a lot, and she'd felt free. This me... felt trapped, lost, and afraid.

"I love you," he whispered in my ear, before he pulled away. I smiled.

He winked at me.

We'd had a lot of sex this week. It had been another of his ways of reassuring me, we hadn't done it much for a while before that.

"Morning, Rachel," his mom called. She was cooking pancakes. The scent of them filled the kitchen.

I didn't want to leave here, or Saint. This was home. But Jason and I had to go. If we didn't, Saint would leave us.

Maybe I'd explode, suddenly, the weight pressing down on me was so heavy. Jason took Saint from my arms and hugged him. I didn't know if I was well enough to go to New York. I didn't know if I'd cope.

But I knew some things; I didn't want to have to deal with Declan when the doctors had me all drugged up and knocked out like a zombie, I couldn't carry on as I was, and I couldn't let Declan take Saint.

Those things had to change.

I had to stop them happening.

CHAPTER TWO

Rachel

My fingers held on to the arm of the seat as I stared out the window of the small United Airlines plane. It was taxiing out to the runway. My body was so heavy with fear it felt like I'd been tied down to the seat with iron chains. They held me in place. I wanted to run. I could see Saint, in my head, reaching out his hands for me when I'd walked away with Jason. My heart hadn't beaten in a normal pattern since.

But I was doing this for Saint. To protect him. To keep him.

Jason could have gone alone. But I didn't want him to go alone. I didn't want Jason to leave me. I wanted to be with him—but I wanted to be with Saint too. I was breaking in half. The two guys in my life were ripping me in half.

I sighed out. My breath became moisture on the small oval window. My teeth sank into my lower lip, holding in the emotion threatening to well over in a flood of tears as I lifted a hand and wiped the moisture away.

"Are you okay?" Jason's hand rested over mine on the seat arm.

I didn't look at him, just turned my hand up the other way and clasped his, clinging to any connection that held me closer to normal.

"Rach…" He pushed, worry catching in his voice

"Yeah." No. I was a fucked-up mess. But he knew that already.

The plane taxied around, turning on to the runway, then stopped.

I breathed in deep and held the air in my lungs. The image in my head became the packet of meds I'd left in the drawer in our room. The meds I'd stopped taking a week ago. I couldn't be the zombie I was when I took them. I needed my brain to be working. Declan was clever. I needed to be able to think when I faced him. The meds made me feel like I was drowning all the time, trapped under an ocean and looking at the world through a fog; I couldn't breathe through it, or reach through it. I needed to be alive and awake to cope with Declan and New York.

My head was full of memories, memories that said the meds would make everything too hard to deal with—and there was the memory of Jason telling me at the Halloween party the other day that he missed the me who'd had crazy moments. He'd liked my crazy moments. The meds stomped on all my crazy—I wanted to be able to be crazy sometimes. I wanted to make him laugh and smile wide. I wanted to make sure he wouldn't stop loving me.

"It'll be okay," Jason said as the pilot switched up the engine and the plane started speeding along the asphalt highway to the sky. G-force pulled at my stomach, making it queasy.

"Don't worry," Jason reassured again. "It's going to be alright."

I looked at him and tried to smile. He smiled back, closed lipped, but considerate. It wasn't the smile I longed for. Nothing was right. Not now.

I wanted it to be right.

"Sorry, I'm missing Saint."

"I miss him too, so we'll get to New York, sort everything out as fast as we can, and get back. Two weeks. That's what I'm giving us. We have to have this fixed by Thanksgiving."

I nodded.

The nose of the plane lifted, pressing us back into the seats, and then we were off the ground and rising, climbing through the air, up into the sky. I wanted to climb like that in spirit. I wanted my bipolar, spinning-top of a brain to whiz up. I hated the swamp of middle road. I wanted to feel high. I wanted to be buzzing with happiness.

10

Jason's fingers squeezed mine.

I looked back out the window, down at the earth, at the city beneath us, as Portland became like a toy town. Saint was miles away from us already, but soon he'd be hundreds of miles away from us. There was a hook in my heart trying to pull me back. The pain of it became sharper the higher the plane climbed.

We breached the clouds and flew above an ocean of glistening vapor, caught in the brightest sunlight.

"Saint will never remember this, you know. I bet you don't have any memories before you were one… So don't worry about what he's thinking, he's fine with Mom and Dad. They're going to feed him and cuddle him loads, and he's going to be okay."

I was learning to hate the word okay, but I nodded as tears slipped from my eyes while I watched the swirling clouds making patterns below us.

"Hey…" Jason's fingertips touched my cheek and turned my head, then he kissed a tear away. "It's going to be okay." I think he thought if he used the word enough he'd make it happen.

I nodded, then looked back out the window. I didn't feel that in my heart, and he didn't know my ex like I did. Declan had been Jason's boss for a year, but I'd lived with Declan and I knew the darkness that was in him. Jason had only glimpsed it.

I didn't see how we could win; Declan had money and contacts and influence. We had us, love for Saint, a sense of right and wrong, and a small-time solicitor in Portland.

The tears tightened into a lump in my throat. If I hadn't messed up we wouldn't be on this flight, we'd be at home with Saint.

Jason lifted my hand and kissed my fingers.

I looked back at him. I was such hard work. I felt sorry for him.

"Hey, we're nearly there. We're over New York."

My eyelids were heavy as I opened them and lifted my head to look at Jason. I'd slept on his shoulder. I was drowsy and there was a density in my body that made my limbs feel like stone. It

11

could be the meds lingering or my mood falling. The meds had made me feel asleep even when I was awake.

Jason gave me a subdued smile. It said what he wouldn't: *I keep telling you it'll all be okay because I know that's what you want to hear, but I'm not convinced.*

I smiled back. He was looking out for me. That's what Jason did, he cared, with a heart that was as big as an ocean.

But our smiles hadn't used to say it'll be alright or I'm sorry— we used to smile because we were happy together.

The seatbelt light was on. I looked down. He'd buckled mine back up while I'd been out of it. I looked out the window. The plane was banking around, flying in over the Upper Bay of the Hudson. I leaned over to look down at the city that had been my home for a large part of my miserable life. I had so many bad memories, memories of me being crazy and stupid, but then I saw the Brooklyn Bridge, and behind it, Manhattan Bridge, as the river's path split. I'd met Jason on Manhattan Bridge, on a night I'd cracked up entirely and decided I'd had enough. Jason had found me there and saved me from myself.

"Brooklyn, Manhattan Bridge, and DUMBO," he said in a low husky voice.

I glanced back at him. He'd remembered the moment I'd met him too. He'd taken me to his apartment in DUMBO that night; we hadn't left each other since. He pressed a quick kiss on my lips, then we both leaned over and looked down, watching the plane come around, following the Hudson, rather than the East river.

I took a breath, a part of me was terrified about coming back and facing Declan, and yet, with my distorted bipolar brain, another part of me experienced a sudden fizz of excitement. New York.

CHAPTER THREE

Jason

I walked out of JFK airport, pulling our suitcase on its wheels and gripping Rach's hand like I was hanging on to her as luggage too. But I felt protective. This trip was scary. Saint's life was hanging on a line, and the other end of it was wrapped around Mr. Rees's finger, and he kept jerking it, messing us around.

I'd worked for him for a year, and thought him an asshole, but then I'd met the side of him Rach knew, when he'd tried to drag her into his car with three other guys, like it was okay to snatch a woman when she didn't want to go. No way did I want him to take Saint. Saint was my son and he might have Mr. Rees's DNA, but that was the only tie he should ever have to that asshole.

We were booked on the SuperShuttle to get out to the hotel. There was a van waiting. I handed over our tickets and stashed our luggage in the back while Rachel waited on the sidewalk. Then we got in. I made sure she was by the window so she didn't have to cope with any strangers too close.

We sat in silence as the van filled up, and stayed silent as it drove through the city. New York. The Big Apple. Rachel looked at the streets as the van dropped people off at the Manhattan hotels. She had more history with New York than I did. I'd never really settled here, my roots and soul had always been back in Oregon. But Rachel had tamed this place and played it for the years she'd lived here. She'd taken a massive bite out of the apple. I'd left it to go rotten. It had never tasted good to me.

Our hotel was in Brooklyn, near the area where I used to live, DUMBO, Down Under the Manhattan Bridge Overpass. The hotel was a narrow, sky-scraping building. It stood out, tall amongst the lower-story buildings surrounding it. We unloaded our stuff and walked into the place.

I guess its whole theme was tall and narrow; the welcome desk area was the same.

I checked us in as Rach stood near me, her arms crossed defensively in front of her chest and her hands clasping either elbow.

The last time I'd checked us into a hotel it had been in Las Vegas, when we'd gotten married.

We were up on the fifteenth floor. Rach pressed the button for the elevator, then stood staring at the numbers above the elevator doors. The doors opened. I lifted a hand encouraging her to go in first. I followed, with the suitcase.

She leaned her shoulders against the wall, so I stood next to her, slid a hand around her and gave her ass a pat to make her smile. She did smile—slightly.

Everything was ruined. She never gave me bright smiles anymore, and it was all Mr. Rees's fault. She'd been fine until he'd started messing us around over Saint. First off, before all of this, he wouldn't do the DNA test and I'd needed him to do it so I could start the adoption process. That was about the time she'd walked into the river with Saint. So then I'd come to New York, alone, and forced him into doing the fucking DNA test. Only since then he'd stopped not wanting Saint and started sharpening fucking knives to chuck at us.

Our room was alright, nothing special. It had a desk in front of a mirror outside the en suite, a chest of drawers, a king-sized bed with a nightstand either side and a long window which looked out across the city. Rach walked over to the window as I lifted the suitcase up on to a stool.

"This reminds me of your apartment." She turned back and looked at me.

"Yeah." It did a little. I'd had a floor-length window like that; it had looked out over DUMBO.

She looked back out.

I walked up behind her, slid my hands over her belly and kissed her neck. "What do you want to do, go out?"

Her head fell back on to my shoulder. "I don't know."

I missed my Rachel, the vibrant, half-crazy girl I'd met. She was smothered by her meds. But she'd been vulnerable then too, and lonely, and easily hurt behind all her bravado. She had crashed down into sad moods as fast as she'd gotten happy and dragged me into doing something I'd have avoided like hell if it hadn't been for her.

I'd been reading up on bipolar on the internet, though, and she might need to be on her strong meds right now, but people didn't have to stay on heavy doses forever, they reduced them. She'd get back to herself one day. Soon, I hoped. "Then let's walk down to the Brooklyn Bridge Park?"

She turned around and pressed her face into my neck. Her lips touched my skin when she said, "I'd like that."

"I thought you might." It was one of our old haunts. We had memories there.

I pressed her back against the window and kissed her properly. Her arms lifted up on to my shoulders and rested there as her tongue wove about mine slowly. My hands slid to grip her butt and I pulled her hips against mine.

Many things had gone wrong in our marriage in the last few months, but the one thing we'd recently managed to fix was the sex. We'd been to a party a week ago, for Halloween, and gone outside in the dark. But then she'd told me about this threat from Mr. Rees.

15

I broke away from her. "Come on, let's go to the park."

I got the first proper smile I'd had out of her all day. Those smiles were way too rare.

We walked through Brooklyn holding hands. Then headed into the park and looked up at the massive bridge, with Manhattan Bridge as its shadow. I let go of her hand and slung my arm around her shoulders.

The Brooklyn Bridge was a giant. It dwarfed us. I'd forgotten how dominating the New York skyline was. It put you in your place, made you realize how much of a nothing you were in the world. That's how I'd always felt in New York.

We walked along the path by the river.

This park was so familiar and yet we'd been different people when we'd been here last. She'd poured out her sordid past to me here, the night I'd found out about Saint. But that had been in the dark. We'd generally come here in the dark after I'd picked her up from work, when all the lights were reflected on the water, swaying with the rock of the waves. It was a different place in the daylight and there were more people here, tourists as well as locals.

When we were far enough away from the main tourist area, I stopped and held the railing, looking down at the water as it washed up against the bank.

Rach gripped the rail too.

I looked at her.

Her gaze stretched to the far bank. "When will we go and see Declan?"

"Monday, so we can have tomorrow to do normal stuff before we face him."

She turned around and looked at me. "What will you say?"

"I have no idea. It depends on what he says… and what he's like."

"An asshole." A smile parted her lips as she quoted back what I'd called him for the year he was my boss.

I chucked her under the chin. "That I can guarantee. He's always that. Shall we walk up to Manhattan Bridge?" Where I'd found her, alone, destitute, and desperate. "Then I thought we could go and eat at Joe's, where you used to work."

She leaned forward and kissed my cheek. "Thanks, I'd like that."

It was nearly a year since I'd found her in a tee and jeans, she'd had nothing else on but her sneakers, on a freezing night in New York.

A subway train passed as we reached the DUMBO end of the Manhattan Bridge's path. It rattled along on the rails, making a racket. I'd used to deaden the sound with the music in my earphones when I'd jogged along here. We didn't walk out very far on to the bridge, but we walked along the path until we saw where she'd been the night I met her. She caught hold my fingers and turned away from it. "Can we walk back past where you used to live? Some of those days were my happiest."

Her words cut, but she hadn't meant them to cut—it's just—I wished she was happy now. She should be happy now. I needed to make her happy again.

Joe, the restaurant owner, her old boss, made a fuss of her when we went in there. Rach was really pretty and one of those girls that when you met her you didn't forget her; so even though she'd only worked there for a few weeks, Joe and the others remembered her. But the thing was, that when we'd lived here, what had made her memorable had been the light of joy and mischief that had shone out of her. That light had gotten snuffed out by her meds.

Sitting in the restaurant, remembering how she used to be, made me miss that girl more than ever. But then, maybe this was who she was really—the person who wasn't sick—and I had to just suck it up and get used to it.

She'd have to get used to it too, though, and she wasn't coping so well with it either. She was scared I'd stop loving her now that she was different.

17

I'd spent the last seven days proving to her just how much in love with her I still was. I still was... But it was painful loving her now, not an exciting rush. My heart hurt and my head was a mess—and I hoped when everything was fixed with Mr. Rees it would all calm down, and she and I, we could just be us again.

When we got back to the room, Rach dropped her purse on the bed, then bent over and took out her cell. "I'm gonna call Mom and speak to Saint."

"It's too late."

She looked at the clock by the bed. It showed eleven-thirty in red digits.

Her expression crumbled in distress.

Ah shit. Now she'd kick herself that she hadn't called earlier. She'd be telling herself she was a bad mom.

Tears flooded her eyes, making the unusual soft mossy green sharpen and sparkle in the electric light. "Why didn't you tell me?"

Because I'd thought about it and decided it was best to let her settle in here and do normal stuff for an afternoon and we hadn't eaten dinner alone since Saint had been born.

I caught hold of her hands before they could lift and clasp her hair. I hated that pose. She'd been in that pose for all the days she'd been in the hospital, when they'd put her on the shitty meds she was taking now. "Hey. It's okay not to speak to him for a day. We'll call first thing in the morning."

"But why didn't I think to call earlier?"

"Because you've got a ton of stuff going on in your head. You were thinking about facing Declan and coming back to New York."

"But I should think of Saint first. Why don't I think of him first?"

"Because you're on a load of meds..." *and your bipolar brain just doesn't work like that, sweetheart.*

Rach had always been scared she'd turn out like her mom,

who'd been so crap at motherhood Rach had run away at fifteen, and since Rach had walked into the river she didn't trust herself at all. She challenged everything she thought, and why she thought it, or more frequently didn't think it. She was trying to make her brain work like normal. But Rach wasn't normal, and that was one of the reasons I'd fallen for her.

She hadn't tried to drown Saint anyway, she'd been thinking of him and trying to teach him to swim. She'd walked into the water with him to swim with him. Fully clothed, yeah. But she'd just lost her hold on reality in a moment of distorted euphoria. That happened with bipolar. It wasn't because she was a bad mom.

Rach started to cry. I pulled her into a hug and stroked a hand over her hair. "He's okay."

"Why didn't you remind me? You aren't on meds!" She pushed me away and smacked my shoulder.

"Because he's with Mom and Dad. He's fine."

Her eyes accused me of not loving Saint enough.

She challenged me as much as herself. She challenged everything lately. She'd been bruised inside by her error. But she was really sick and the meds they'd given her to make her better were making her judgments even more distorted. So I was letting her get away with insecurity and accusations against me, but I wouldn't lie, they cut.

She broke away from me, turned, moved her purse over on to a shelf beside the bed, then collected her stuff from the suitcase and disappeared into the bathroom. Her movements had been hurried and twitchy with anger. When she came back in she was wearing a t-shirt only and she'd wiped off her make-up, ready to get into bed.

I went into the bathroom and got ready too. I washed my face and stared at myself in the mirror. It had been a long year. My life had turned around completely.

When I went back into the bedroom, I stripped off my jeans

and my tee, but left my boxers on. I switched off the main light, then got into bed, and switched off the lamp on the nightstand. "Do I get a cuddle?" I said into the darkness.

"Yeah."

I lifted my arm and she shuffled over and leaned on my shoulder. But I figured it wasn't a night for sex. I wasn't getting that vibe from her.

CHAPTER FOUR

Rachel

Sunlight poured through the transparent curtains. Jason was sitting on the bed, looking at me, and the TV was on. "What?" I breathed from a croaky throat.

"It's eleven-thirty; you've had twelve hours' sleep."

He knew what that meant. It meant my mood had dropped. I was morose and tired when my mood was low—but it didn't have to mean the meds were wearing off, the meds made me sleepy anyway.

"Do you want to call Saint, then go for a run?" He also knew that running was a good trigger for helping me lift my mood.

I sat up. "I'd like to call Mom and speak to Saint." Jason was fully clothed in running gear, he looked like he'd been up for ages waiting for me to wake up. He got up and walked over to pick my cell up from the nightstand, then threw it on to the bed next to me.

My heart raced as I looked up Mom and Dad's number. An image of Saint hovered in my head, the one of him laughing for the first time last week. I touched the call icon for their home number. It rang about five times as my heart pounded out the seconds.

"Hello. This is Mrs. Macinlay."

"Hi, Mom."

"Rachel. How are you?"

"We're okay. We walked around where Jason used to live last night. Is Saint okay?"

"Yes, dear, he's fine."

"Did he sleep okay?"

"Yes, all through the night. We've put him in our room as he's used to sleeping in with you and Jason."

"Thanks..." I sighed the word out in relief. Saint was okay. Yet... What if he didn't miss me because I was such a crappy mom? That thought made me want him not to be okay, but that made me feel more of a shitty mom. "Could you put the phone to his ear?"

"He's with Grampy, wait a moment, I'll take the phone to them." The line was silent for a while then she said, "Here you are."

I heard breathing. "Saint, it's Mommy. Hello, sweetheart." There was a slight catch in his breath, that said he knew my voice.

Jason came over to the bed and bent down near my cell. "It's Daddy too."

"I miss you. I love you," I whispered into the cell.

"We miss you and we love you," Jason said loudly, before he straightened up.

Why did I keep judging Jason badly? He was here to fight for Saint. He wanted to adopt Saint. Of course he loved him too. If I kept doubting him, I was going to push him away. I had to stop my head from doubting him.

His mom came back on. "Saint was smiling and listening like he was trying to work out where you were in the room."

"Give him lots of cuddles and kisses from us. I'll call again tonight."

"Okay, call as often as you want, and we're going to cuddle him all day long." Jason's mom had become my mom too. She was really patient with my weirdness and paranoia.

"Thank you. Bye."

"Goodbye, Rachel, give our love to Jason." The call went dead.

I looked up at him. "She sends you their love. Saint smiled."

Jason smiled at me, with his mouth shut. I wanted him to give me a big full-on broad smile. I wanted to smile like that too—I wanted my meds to wear off so that I could smile like that again.

"I'll get up and go running with you." I threw the comforter back. I had to walk past him because the room wasn't very wide. He smacked my ass.

"Good girl."

I glanced at him over my shoulder. The smile pulling at my lips had a warmth that came from my belly. Maybe my meds had started wearing off.

I turned around and looked at him. "I'm sorry I shouted at you last night."

"It's okay, you're forgiven." He shrugged it off.

We ran down to Prospect Park, one of the places we used to run when I'd lived with him here. I hadn't run with him for weeks and it meant he had to go a lot slower, but Jason had never cared about that, he'd always made it clear he liked running with me.

Just by living with him, I held him back—but he kept saying he didn't care.

Blood pulsed in my arteries and my muscles flooded with energy, as the sounds of the city absorbed and consumed me while we ran: cars, cabs, people. Jason had his earphones in, but I hadn't put any music on, I was just running to the heartbeat of New York.

When we got into the park, the noisy sounds of the city drifted into the distance and the closer noise became the birds amidst the jewel-like colors of the leaves on the trees that had changed for the fall, and there were kids and some guys playing a game of baseball. We ran a circuit around the park, then ran back to the hotel, I was breathing hard when we arrived and I doubled over in the elevator trying to get my breath back, but it was a good sort of breathless.

Jason had pulled out his earphones and they dangled from his neck, still playing music.

"What are you listening to?"

He gave me a smile that was a little wider than any other smile I'd had from him today. "The compilation you gave me last Christmas."

I straightened up as a sound of humor slipped out of my throat. I smiled at him with parted lips. I loved him so much, it gripped in my belly as well as my chest and sent a tingle through my nerves into my muscles, that were warm from running.

When we reached our room and shut the door behind us it was like we shut out the world.

He'd said on Halloween we'd become us again because we'd had risky sex in the garden.

Now I felt like we'd become us again.

He took his cell out of his pocket and put it on the nightstand, then stripped off his sweaty top and tee. He was good to look at, his body did stuff to my belly too, and what it did to my belly was as powerful as what his love did to my heart, but this feeling didn't touch my heart. I smiled even wider at him when he turned around and flashed his sinewy, sculpted abdomen at me.

"What?" he asked of my smile.

"Nothing. Are you gonna have a shower?"

"Yeah."

"Can I get in with you?"

"Yeah." He sent a smile, like mine, right back at me.

I pulled off my top as he stripped off his jogging pants and walked into the bathroom naked. I heard the shower turn on as I undid my bra. I took my panties off, then headed for the bathroom.

He'd pulled the shower curtain halfway across the bath, so I could still get in around it. He was standing under the stream of water, with his back to me, letting the water run over his short hair. His hand lifted and brushed across his head. I stepped over

24

the side of the bath and moved forward. My hands settled on his lean hips, then slid down, my thumbs following the curve of his tight butt.

He turned and then his hand was at the back of my head and his lips came down on to mine. I opened my mouth to press my tongue into his, but he beat me to it, his tongue passing through my lips. I sucked it slightly then bit it gently. A growl left his throat, then his hands were at the back of my thighs, just below my bottom. My arms wrapped around his neck so he could lift me.

He pressed me against the tiles as he slid into me, filling me up with a hard, slow pressure.

I kissed his temple and he bit my neck when he withdrew and pressed back in.

His palms held under my thighs, his fingertips pressing into my muscle.

One of my hands clasped the back of his neck, while the other grasped at his shoulder. "Jason," I said into his ear. All the sex we'd been having in the last week made me feel as though we were clinging to sex, trying to reclaim what had been normal between us. If we had nothing else right between us—we had gotten the sex back to being right.

He shoved into me, over and over, working hard. Working like he loved sex with me, not just loved me.

My orgasm exploded in a swell of sensation, and I cried out. Jason growled and bit my shoulder. I laughed. He just thrust into me harder, glancing down to watch, then he looked back up, right into my eyes.

From the moment I'd met him, I'd had a weird connection to him—or maybe I'd just fancied the hell out of him. But I'd always known we were meant to be together.

My butt and my back bumped against the tiles as the water fell on our sides. I laughed—but it was strange—fake. It came from my throat not my belly.

25

He kissed my lips. My hand slid up and cradled the back of his head, holding his mouth to mine so we kept kissing as he pressed hard into me over and over until I came again. Then he came with a deep, long sigh that released into my mouth.

He smiled at me, with his lips closed. But, this smile, softened the look of his eyes too and his gaze said, *I love you*. He was the fixer, he was working hard to fix us, and he was doing it the only way he probably knew how, with sex. I loved him more for trying to heal what had broken in me. He could have chosen to walk away.

He could still choose to walk away. Most guys would.

He withdrew from me, then lowered my legs. "Shall we go to Times Square after we've showered?"

"Yeah. I'd like that." It was where he'd proposed to me, after Christmas, last year. In a few weeks we'd have been married a year.

We washed each other's hair, ran soapy hands over each other's bodies, then washed ourselves off under the stream of water, switched it off and stepped out.

While Jason was drying himself with one towel, I wrapped mine around me and picked up my cell.

"Hey, don't tell me you're going to call Mom because you didn't think about Saint while we were having sex?"

A blush flooded my skin. Because that was why.

"He's okay, and it's okay not to think about him for half an hour, it doesn't make you a bad mom."

But the fear that I was, was part of the one-ton weight pushing me down, and the iron chains holding me there.

I pressed the call icon to ring Mom and Dad.

I didn't sleep so well, I was drifting in and out of dreams again tonight. Declan was in them, and Jason, and we were in New York with Saint.

Saint was in the river with me, in the deep water of the Hudson.

26

Then I was on Manhattan Bridge in the dark, watching the lights on the shifting water and gripping the grill, getting ready to climb it so I could jump.

I'd have drowned in that water, if I'd jumped from Manhattan Bridge.

The water was cold and dirty, it sucked me under, dragging me down, and then Saint was in my arms, and it was dragging us both down, and trying to pull him away. Declan's face jeered at me in the murky cold.

"Rach…" Jason's hand touched my back.

My eyes opened on a moment of another memory, of his hand touching my back the night I'd been climbing the grill, to jump off the bridge. He'd talked me out of it and taken me home with him. "I was dreaming," I whispered without lifting my head off the pillow I'd made of his chest.

"I know, and it didn't sound all that good."

"Nope."

"The river…"

"Yeah, that and Declan."

His arm came around me and his hand squeezed my shoulder. "It'll be okay."

That was what he kept saying. But it was Declan we were going up against. Declan didn't do okay. He did nasty, mean, and cruel. Never okay. Okay as an aim, or a desire, was mediocre. It was losing to Declan. He didn't do anything without putting all his influence behind it. He didn't lose. I wanted things to be awesome.

My palm settled on Jason's bare belly as his breathing slowed and shifted into the soft rhythm of sleep.

I couldn't sleep.

Maybe my meds were wearing off.

CHAPTER FIVE

Jason

I ran a finger along Rach's forearm as it rested on top of the covers, to wake her. "Hey, someone wants to say hi to you."

Her eyes opened, looking at me. She'd been in a deep sleep even though it was already eleven a.m.

"I face-timed Dad, it's Saint." I held my iPhone out so she could see him and he'd be able to see her.

She lifted up on to her elbows, smiling instantly. "Saint."

"He says, good morning, Mommy."

"Good morning, sweetheart. What are you doing?"

"Playing with Grampy, he's had his second bottle of milk today and he's full of beans." Dad's voice came through the cell.

Saint was making sweet, babbling, I'm-full-up, happy sounds and he was laying on his back while his legs and arms kicked out like he was doing a little kickboxing routine.

She took the cell out of my hand. "Did Grampy change your diaper?"

"Grampy did not, that is Granny's task."

She'd been teasing him about his dislike of diapers since Saint had been born. It was good to hear the humor in her voice. She'd been lacking humor since she'd been on her meds. It was a ray of the Rachel I'd fallen for in the beginning, shining through the gray clouds of the last couple of months.

"So you let Grampy do all the fun bits and leave all the nasty sick and poo to Granny… That's not fair, Saint, Granny wants playtime too."

I laughed and tumbled down on the bed beside her, so Saint could see me. But really Rach had to get up, we needed to go. "Dad, we need to get into the office, so I'm going to have to chase Rach out of bed. Saint, say goodbye to Mommy." Dad's hand came into view and lifted Saint's hand to wave at us. Saint made the cutest baby face, with a toothless smile.

I loved my kid. His blood might not be mine, but it didn't matter, he was my son. I wanted to adopt him, but if I hadn't been pushing to make him legally mine then maybe we could've lived together forever in peace and avoided Mr. Rees paying any attention to us. He wouldn't have had any reason for this custody fight.

I reckoned this mess was my fault.

"Bye." Rach pressed a kiss on to her fingertips then blew it off them toward the screen.

I pursed my lips and blew Saint a smacker. "Bye, Saint. Bye, Dad. We'll call you later."

"Yes, bye, Rachel. Goodbye, son."

I pressed the end-call icon, then took the cell out of her hand. "Okay, Rachel Macinlay, you need to get up and we need to go and fight for our kid."

She gave me a smile, which was not the reaction I'd expected. "What time did you get up?"

"Two hours ago." I'd washed, dressed, and just been looking out the window playing games on my cell ever since, leaving her to sleep because I knew she'd had a bad night, dreaming. Off meds Rach had two extremes: never sleeping and sleeping nearly all day and night, but on the meds she was just always a little bit doped up. I hated her meds more than she did, probably, and that was saying something, but I felt like they were crushing her. She wasn't anything close to normal on her meds.

I sighed—remembering again that, maybe, who she was now was normal for the not-mentally-sick Rach.

29

But that was why I'd made another call this morning, before I'd called Mom and Dad, because I needed to know what was right and what was wrong, and so many things didn't feel right at the moment.

I got up off the bed when she walked into the bathroom. "I called the hospital here this morning!"

She reappeared, holding the door jamb and looking at me, her eyes questioning. "Why?"

"Because, first of all, it would be good for you to have two psychologists to make a statement for you if we end up in a courtroom before a judge fighting to keep Saint and, second of all, because I thought the guy here talked a lot of sense when we saw him last year, and I want you to have a second opinion on the best treatment for you. You don't feel good on the meds you're taking, and maybe there's some other choice."

"You made an appointment already…"

"Yeah, for the end of next week."

She turned away and walked into the bathroom, not giving me a clue what she thought about what I'd done. There'd been nothing in her body language and I hadn't seen her expression.

I sighed and turned around, there was no point in following her in there to push her for a response. Rachel shared things when she wanted, and not when she didn't. I left her to get her head around the idea. My head was full anyhow. I was getting my brain around what the hell to say to Mr. Rees to stop him pushing for custody. No ideas had come to me yet.

How did I win against a rich guy who could afford billion-dollar lawyers?

I didn't even really get why he was fighting… He hadn't wanted Saint to be born. He'd wanted Rach to have an abortion. I still had his stupid scribbled note saying he didn't want anything to do with the kid if she had it.

So why had he changed his mind?

Because I wanted Saint…

That's what I thought, that this was between him and me and had nothing to do with Rach or Saint. They'd just gotten caught up in it. When I'd worked for him he'd seen me as a nobody and neither of us had known about our connection when I'd found Rach and she'd moved in with me. It wasn't until the party he'd had when I saw her picture in his penthouse that I found out who Rach's abusive ex had been—my boss.

I'd quit work. I'd heard enough about her ex from Rach to know there was no way I could work for him knowing that, especially when we were going to raise his kid.

But after I'd walked out of work, he'd come after Rach. He'd turned up at my place, late at night, off his head on something, with a group of guys. That hadn't been just about Rach. He'd wanted to take her away from me, not just take her. I'd been the guy he'd deemed a worthless piece of shit. He had loads of money. Several businesses. Friends in powerful places. Massive houses. The best of everything. Everything I could never hope for. But I'd kicked his ego that night I'd blackened his eye and probably broken his rib, and he'd gone away. I'd won that night.

But Mr. Rees was the sort of guy who didn't like losing.

Shit.

So how did I persuade a man like that to let us keep Saint and stop fighting?

I didn't know. But I was trying to convince Rach I did. I'd told her everything was going to be okay. That we'd get this fixed. But the problem was—I looked at my watch and remembered how long it used to take me to get to the office, about forty-five minutes—in forty-five minutes she was going to discover that I'd lied.

Nausea twisted around in my gut and I rubbed my hands on the seat of my pants.

I'd hated the asshole a year ago, but that feeling then had been a shallow dislike. Now it was a violent distaste. But the cutting thing was, that underneath every feeling I had, I still had this

31

shitty sense he was better than me, because he had so much more than I did.

"What do you want to wear?" I shouted into the bathroom. I had to do something other than stand here, otherwise I was going to blow like a volcano of nervous energy. I would've run while Rach was sleeping but I didn't want to leave her to wake up alone.

"My light jeans, my dark-blue long-sleeved tee and my pale-blue sweater!"

"Okay, I'll get them out of the suitcase."

"You can pick my underwear!"

The first day we'd been out together, nearly a year ago, the first trip we'd made was shopping for clothes for her. She'd left Mr. Rees with nothing but the clothes she'd had on at the time, which hadn't included underwear. She'd waved the underwear at me as she'd picked it, with a laugh. I wanted to hear that laugh right now.

I chose blue underwear, to go with the clothes she'd picked, and then laid all her clothes out on the bed. She came out of the bathroom, naked and smiling at me.

I hadn't expected her to be smiling this morning, and it may not be a wide smile, just a lifting at the corner of her lips, but she was definitely smiling.

She dressed while I sat on the bed watching, with my palms on my thighs, trying to restrain the anxiety that whipped at my back. I didn't want to let it show. When she turned and slipped her cell into her purse, I stood up. "Are you ready?" I wasn't, but there was no running from this standoff, it had to happen.

She turned and gave me another slight smile. "Yeah."

What was with her smiling today?

We put our coats on, ready for the cold walk to the subway, then went out the door. My hand settled at her waist and I kept my arm around her as we travelled down in the elevator, and when we walked out the door of the hotel her arm came

32

around me and her hand slipped into the back pocket of my pants.

We were tight together—right. Declan and Rachel... they'd been so wrong.

We had to stand in the subway car. I grasped the bar over my head as she leaned back against an upright one with her hands behind her, her body rocking with the sway of the car. She didn't look like she was scared at all. But I knew she was scared of Mr. Rees, of what he'd done to her, and what he might do yet. Maybe she was hiding her fear like I was.

When we got off the subway I held her hand through her woolen glove. Her hand hung on tightly to mine as we made our way out of the station, and then walked to the office where I used to work. For months I'd walked this route, and I'd only been glad to be walking it for about the first two weeks, when I'd still had hopes it would be the dream job I'd wanted. It had never been that. I hadn't been sorry at all to leave it behind for Rach.

When we got nearer the office, my nerves ratcheted up ten notches. I couldn't take her in there. What if it went badly? It was better if I did this alone.

There was a Starbucks near the office. I stopped in front of it. "Do me a favor, Rach, wait here, please? I don't want to take you in there."

Her hand slipped out of mine and she faced me, clasping the sleeves of my leather jacket instead and trying to shake me. "Why?"

My hands settled at her hips. "Because the man is unpredictable, nasty, and violent."

"I know him better than you do." Her words turned into a cloud of mist in the cold winter air.

"You do. But we both know this isn't going to be fixed by me speaking to him once. Just let me go in there alone and judge the ground."

She sighed. She hated being shut out of anything.

When she looked down I held her head and kissed her forehead, then when she looked up I kissed her cheek and then her lips. "Do as I ask," I said over her mouth, looking into her eyes, "please..."

Maybe it was for my benefit, because I was scared how things were going to go down, but I told myself it was for her, because I'd seen the way he treated her the way he twisted her emotionally.

Her gloved hands shook me, through her grip on my jacket, expressing her frustration. "I don't want to let you do it alone."

"But you will..."

Her mouth and forehead twisted in a grimace of dislike, but her lips spoke the word I wanted to hear. "Yeah."

I breathed out with relief.

"But I hate the idea—for the record."

I gave her a smile, then pressed my forehead against hers for an instant. "It's noted, sweetheart. But I'd hate taking you in there more than you hate the idea of being outside."

She pulled back, annoyed again. "I said I'd wait here."

"I won't be long."

"Don't be." Her words snapped at me.

I leaned forward quickly and pressed another kiss on her lips. She opened her mouth and my quick kiss became a little hot for the middle of a sidewalk, but inappropriate was part of me and Rach.

When I broke the kiss, she smiled, her lips parting. What was with her smiles? I'd been expecting another sullen face, sulking over having to stay behind. I smiled back anyway and chucked her under the chin. "Give me half an hour, maybe a little bit more."

"Okay."

"See you in a while."

"Okay."

I pressed my lips on to hers, this time it was quickly, then let her go, as she let me go. "Bye."

"I'll be waiting for you."

My heart fucking pounded like crazy when I turned to face the office farther along the street. I breathed out, steeling myself to go in there and face this.

It was lunchtime, so the building's reception area was busy. I ignored the elevators and headed for the stairs. I jogged up, my teeth gritting.

Memories hit me in the face.

But the memories weren't from when I'd worked here, they were from when I'd come back here to get Mr. Rees's DNA, after Rach had walked into the river. I'd been a wreck. My head had been totally fucked up. I'd been scared. I'd never seen her have an extreme episode until that night, and when I'd left her in the hospital in Portland she'd been oblivious to the world, cradling herself and silent. She'd barely known me.

Those images had been in my head when I'd walked into the office then; they were in my head now.

The fear I'd carried around with me for weeks after that episode hovered inside me; it was all knotted up, a massive rope coiled and tangled up in my belly and my chest, along with the excruciating pain I'd discovered that came when you loved someone who was hurting and you couldn't do anything to help them.

Rachel needed the pressure off her; she needed an end to this—shit. I was the one who'd brought this down on us; if I didn't want to adopt Saint... But giving up now would let Mr. Rees win, and I didn't want him to win, I wanted Saint to be mine. I didn't want to give up, even if that would mean Mr. Rees backing off.

I pushed open the door that led into the area in front of the office.

A new emotion swayed around in me; guilt as well as fear and pain.

"Jason!"

Shit.

Mr. Rees was right in front of me. Staring at me. The wolf

was out of his den and waiting for the elevator doors to open. His personal assistant, Preppy-Portia, stood beside him with a notebook in her hand. He must have been laying out his orders on how to conquer the world, super-villain-style, and she'd been scribbling it all down until I'd walked in on them.

My teeth clenched. Just the sight of him turned my stomach.

"I didn't expect to see you back in New York…" His tone and his body language said he knew he was winning.

Shit… I wasn't prepared for him. I'd gotten caught off guard. My belly screwed up in a tight mess.

Don't take any crap from him. I breathed out, then breathed in, about to speak, but before I could he walked past Portia, grabbed the arm of my jacket and pulled me out into the stairwell.

I guess he didn't want me speaking in front of her.

The guy had a weakness.

As soon as we were through the door, I yanked my arm free. I needed to be in control. "Why are you trying to get custody of Saint?" I stepped forward, to get up in his face. Offence was the best defense. Which was maybe another reason why he'd dragged me out here. But he needed to know I was going to fight him all the way, with whatever it took, no matter that I didn't have the money he had.

He leaned back, as offhand and fucking self-confident as ever, just like I smelled bad. Like I hadn't rattled him at all. "Because I can."

My hands fisted. "You don't want him! Why bother?" It would be easy to hit him out here. It made it harder to hold back. How could he be so fucking calm? He was destroying our lives, destroying the life of a little kid, and he didn't give a shit.

"Because maybe I don't want you to have him more than I don't want him."

He was an asshole. But if he was telling the truth it meant this was my fault!

I opened my hands, fighting the anger and pain as hard as I

wanted to hit him. "Just give this up. This is a kid—a human being. You're playing with him. It's not a game."

"I'm not playing." His fixed, serious expression said, *and you'd better believe it.*

Rage sliced through me, like a knife cut me in half. It took a lot to make me mad, but he made me growl at him, "Stop it! You don't fucking want him!" They'd probably heard me shouting in the office, certainly Portia had heard me if she was still standing by the elevators and she loved to gossip, so she'd be there. If no one else had heard it, they'd hear about it from her.

The sound echoed up and down the stairs.

"No…" The word was spoken like a question, in a low tone. It was said to push my anger harder.

I pictured myself grabbing the knot of his tie and twisting it so hard he choked.

I wanted to kick him in the balls to give him maximum pain, and smash my fists into his face.

But if I did any of that he'd win. That was what he wanted.

A deep breath pulled into my lungs as my fists clenched again. I didn't throw any punches, but I remembered what it had felt like when I'd been in the dark street outside my apartment, late at night, when he'd come to take Rach. Then I'd had justification. But if I did it here he'd have me on an assault charge, and even more evidence to take Saint.

"What the fuck will you gain by doing this?" My voice echoed, shouting back at me.

"Pissing you off." His quiet answer didn't carry, but it hit me like a cold bucket of water.

Awesome. I hated him. My arm lifted in anger and desperation to stop him being a bastard. But I couldn't hit him and I didn't have any power to stop him. I slapped a useless hand on the stair rail then hung on to it. "And what will you fucking do if you win? It'll piss you off too. You wouldn't want Saint with you. Just back off. Leave him with us!"

37

Was he really going through this process just for revenge because Rach had walked out and I'd hit him? But if he took Saint, it was for a lifetime. Would he really do that just to piss me off? Where would Saint end up?

I didn't get this.

"No." The refusal rang with determination. "I've lost my family. My wife saw the paternity paperwork. I've lost the house on the coast," his eyebrows lifted, "and she's after my businesses. Why should you get what you want?"

Shit. His marriage had broken up. That had me reeling back. His money came from his wife. "I didn't trash your marriage, if your shit's exploded, it's because you did it! You cheated! And now you're going to take a child you don't want and dump him on a nanny! That's crazy!"

He leaned toward me. "Rachel's the crazy bitch. Now get out of here or I'll call security." As soon as the last word left his mouth he turned his back on me, pulled the door open, and went back into the elevator area, leaving me alone.

Fuck. It was time to get out.

My hands shook when I jogged down the stairs. I wanted to puke, and every muscle was tight with emotion. I had my hands tied behind my back, powerless. I couldn't be powerless; I had to win.

But at least now I understood why he wanted to fight and maybe I could work out from that how to fight back.

I shoved the door open and walked into the ground-floor reception area. It swung shut heavily behind me. The temper in me brewed up like bubbling lava. I wasn't going to be able to hold it in much longer. I shoved hard with both hands to open the door out into the street.

Anger ricocheted through me. I hadn't gotten any good news to share with Rach and I hadn't been in control of the conversation. But I think Rach and me both knew this wouldn't be solved by me telling him to stop. He was not the sort of person to do

38

anything anyone asked him, for any reason, even if the life and happiness of a kid—his kid—would be ruined... *My kid*. Those two words breathed through my soul.

"He's my kid!" The people I walked past turned and stared as I shouted it out, venting the lava.

Rach was sitting at a table by the window in Starbucks, so she could see me coming. When she did she leaned up against the pane and made a weird face at me, contorting her nose and mouth while she breathed out to mist up the glass. Ah shit. What a moment for a glimmer of the old Rach to shine through her meds. I smiled as I walked in and against all the odds a humorous sound gathered in my throat as I went over to the table. I leaned down and kissed her cheek, because she was mine too, and the emotion stirring like fire in my chest was all for her and Saint. I was holding on to them both, pulling them through this. "I need a coffee. Do you want another?"

"Yeah."

But while I was pulling them through, I was drowning under the pressure... Like I had them both hanging on around my neck, strangling me as I tried to swim and breathe. What if we didn't win? What would happen to Saint? And what would happen to her? I'd been shit today. I wasn't strong enough to win. I didn't have the power to change this.

I sighed out when I turned away, shoving those thoughts aside, as hard as I'd shoved the office doors open to get out of there.

When I walked toward the counter, it was a chance for my manically pumping heart to slow down. I breathed slowly to get control of my heart rate and my temper. She must've been able to tell from my attitude that things had gone badly. But I was glad she'd let me walk away and hadn't pushed to know what had happened. I needed time to get my head back in the right gear, so I could be upbeat with her.

My hand tapped against my leg as I waited on my order and

breathed deeply. I let all the swear words I wanted to yell fly around in my head. Fuck! Bullshit!

When I took our drinks over, I put hers down, then sat facing her. My hands wrapped around the cup. I sighed out my breath. Her green eyes looked deep into mine, wanting answers. She hadn't asked but she wanted to know.

"His marriage broke up. His claim for Saint is revenge. He thinks his marriage breakup is our fault. His money came from his wife, initially, so guess what, his divorce is hitting him hard in the pocket and that's our fault too. She found out about the paternity case."

Rach nodded—then smiled.

What the hell was with her smiles? She was not right today.

My heart pumped harder again, with worry. Ever since the thing with the river I'd been tiptoeing about on broken glass, scared it was going to happen again and not knowing what to do to stop it. Everything weird she did set me on edge. But when she didn't do weird stuff and she was unsmiling and dopey, I feared she'd be forever like that and the Rachel I'd fallen for was lost—along with her old highs and lows. What I wanted was confusing. Just as confusing as she was.

"Jason!"

Shit. I looked over my shoulder to see Justin walking in with Portia. Awesome. We should have gone to another place farther away from the office. Justin had at one time been the only friend I had in New York, and he worked for Mr. Rees too. I hadn't spoken to him since I'd left New York. I'd cut all my ties. I didn't want any connections to anyone around Mr. Rees.

Justin said something to Portia and then, when she joined the queue, he came over, smiling.

Shit.

He must think I was weird. He'd seen me when I came to get Mr. Rees's DNA in the summer. Then I'd gone away again and ignored his texts again.

His gaze shifted from me to Rach.

His eyes widened.

He was the worst frickin' gossip, and he'd seen Rach before—at Mr. Rees's apartment, when she'd been shacked up with Mr. Rees, as his mistress. Or probably a better description would be as his sex toy. He'd used her, that was all. For parties and playing.

I'd never told Justin about the link between the woman I'd met and married in a hurry and our boss. When I'd found out, I'd left work the next day the office opened, but since then Justin had seen me shout at Mr. Rees in the summer and he was with Portia, so he'd know what had just happened. What brought a person back to yell at their ex-boss months after they'd left? Nothing. Normally. But nothing about this was normal.

"You're… With her…" He said it like it was an impossible thing.

"Yeah." I answered in the sort of flat tone Mr. Rees used. It said, *so what?*

"That's something." His eyebrows lifted, and his voice changed to one of, well wow, you lucky fucker. He pulled up a chair and dropped down on to it, sitting at our table without asking if we minded.

Seeing as it was too late to say go away… "Justin, this is my wife, Rachel. Rachel, this is Justin, who I used to work with."

"We've met," he said, smiling at her like it was a riot to catch us together.

She didn't remember him.

"Were you the girl he met on the bridge?" From Justin's voice he was as surprised as if I'd walked into the office and punched him in the belly.

"Yeah…" Rach answered, with a pitch that said, why?

"Mr. Rees's girl," Justin said on a low breath. He'd seen her at a New Year's party in Mr. Rees's flash penthouse apartment. It was the one time a year everyone at work had been treated like humans. "Shit. And that paternity case." He looked at me.

41

Great, how did he know about the paternity case? He'd put the puzzle together.

His eyebrows lifted. "Now everything makes sense. That girl you met on the bridge was pregnant with someone else's kid. I remember. Mr. Rees's fighting you for custody, isn't he?"

"How do you know about the custody thing?" Mr. Rees would not have discussed it. It wouldn't have hit the office gossips' network. Mr. Rees would've hung on to that secret with an armed guard.

Justin's eyebrows lifted again, in the way he'd had of roasting my naivety when I'd been green to New York and sitting at the desk opposite him—the country kid lost in the concrete jungle. "Portia is his Personal Assistant and I'm engaged to her... You accused us of being gossips last time you were here, so you know what the two of us would be like at keeping secrets from each other."

Oh my Lord.

Portia arrived with coffees and sandwiches. Justin got up and pulled another chair over.

It looked like we had their company while we drank our coffee whether we wanted it or not. But I'd liked him a year ago. I hadn't liked Portia so much, though, she'd been pushy, and playing for me, even though she'd known I had a girl.

"This is my wife, Rachel. Rachel, this is Portia from the office." I did the introductions.

"Recognize her..." Justin looked at Portia.

"Ohhh."

Yep, she did.

"The paternity case..." She made the connection too. Awesome.

But then she reached across the table and gripped Rach's hand, which was something I didn't expect. "I'm sorry. It must be awful for you. Mr. Rees is a bastard."

Her preppy, British voice made the statement sound funny. But what I realized, suddenly, was that finally we had some intelligence on Mr. Rees. "What do you know?" I hadn't once thought about Justin, and through him, Portia, being useful.

Rach looked down at Portia's hand; it still held hers, then she looked up into Portia's eyes, asking the question I had, without speaking.

Portia let Rach go and tore open her sandwiches while she spoke. "Most things. I type his letters. His personal ones as well as those for the magazine." She glanced up at me, then looked at Rach. "I know that his wife is suing for divorce because your lawyer sent letters about the baby to his house, so she found out."

"Shit." The word slipped past Rach's lips.

Portia looked at me. "I didn't know the name, but I knew a guy was trying to adopt the kid. It's you, right?"

"Yeah." She knew it all anyway.

"See I told you, now it all makes sense," Justin said in a dry tone. "You coming in before, in the summer, and shouting at him. I thought it was about a reference or something, but that was a bit extreme for someone who gave you a bad rep."

"When did you come in the summer?" Rach looked at me, a little line creasing a frown in her forehead.

My hand lifted and my thumb ran up the line, trying to wipe it away before I answered. "When you were in the hospital. I came to persuade him to do the DNA test, so we could get going with the adoption."

"Oh." The sound said she'd worked out what that meant—that all this shit was my fault.

I looked at Portia. "Do you know everything that he does?"

She nodded. "If it's to do with business, or needs a letter or a phone call."

Or a phone call... I needed to think. What could she find out that would help us? Mr. Rees was a player. There must be some dirty secret he was hiding.

A year ago, his secret had been Rach.

The thought punched me in the gut. I hated to think about

43

her past, and so mostly I didn't, but it was in my face here, I couldn't escape it.

"Would you help us?" I'd never imagined I'd be asking self-obsessed Portia for help. Her crisp, British accent made her sound like she thought herself better than others. But she'd just expressed sympathy to Rach, and Justin liked her, and I'd liked Justin a lot, so by means of elimination, I figured she was worth a chance. Maybe she'd help us.

"How?"

"I don't know, but are you willing if we can think of something? He has evidence against Rach which is giving him the grounds to win custody, the only thing I can think to do is build counter-evidence. He's hardly led a clean life." Portia and Justin made sounds of agreement, Justin's amused, Portia's annoyed. "If we can get some dirt on him, we'd have a chance to fight him. So, will you help?"

"Yeah, I—"

Rach shifted forward in her chair and leaned her elbows on the table, looking hard at Portia. "Does he still take cocaine?" Her voice was sharp, bitter, and accusing. Her mood had swung. The girl who'd made a face at me against the window pane had gone.

"I didn't know he—"

"Does he still invite his powerful friends back to his apartment for sex parties?" Rach's voice said to Portia *you-know-nothing*. But they were from different worlds, and Portia was too well-bred to have a clue about the life Mr. Rees lived behind closed doors.

"No, I… I…didn't know he did that—" If Portia had thought him a bastard already, the shock on her face said she'd happily go back to work and pour arsenic in his coffee.

"Then you don't know much about him," Rach pushed. "I doubt you can help."

Portia's preppy, pitched voice was putting Rach off, like it had me when I'd worked with Portia.

Justin leaned back and wrapped an arm around Portia's shoulders, in a gesture of reassurance that I'd deployed on Rach a million times. "She just wants to help you." He looked at me. He was defending her. They really were tight. As tight as Rach and I… *were.*

The words that had slipped into my head, were *had been.*

It wasn't had been, we were tight. *Are tight.* Good for one another. Right.

"Rach," I breathed, looking at her. "If there's any chance Portia can help… We need all the help we can get."

Rach looked at Portia. Her eyes had been mistrustful. I'd seen the hint of paranoia I'd gotten used to since her brain had been wounded by the river incident.

"Okay. Sure. You can try. But the stuff I said, that's the stuff we need to know about, not about his business conversations."

An image of Portia and the other girls from work going through all of Rach's stuff that she'd left behind at Mr. Rees's place played through my mind's eye. They'd been like vultures, dissecting it all, rooting through every drawer, looking for bikinis to wear in the pool they were going to sneak into, while everyone else carried on the New Year's office party in the living room. That had been less than a year ago. It was hard to believe so much in my life had changed.

But if Portia could help… "Thanks, Portia." I needed some way to get at Mr. Rees. I had to win.

Justin gave me a nod confirming that they'd help, and thanking me for accepting Portia in more ways than her offer of help. He'd known I didn't like her last Christmas. But then his arm slipped off Portia's shoulders and he sat forward. "I know you've ignored every single text from me, but I still have your number, unless you changed it? I can call you if Portia sees or hears anything useful."

I sighed out a breath. This whole thing suddenly seemed like a massive mountain. "We have to work it out quickly, we're here for two weeks, then we have to get back."

"I wanna be with Saint, my son, for Thanksgiving." Rach's voice changed to a pitch of longing when she spoke of Saint.

"Let's get together one evening, then, and throw some ideas around?" Portia suggested. It was Portia's typical let's-get-on-with-it-and-fix-it-all style I'd known at work, and it was probably too much for Rach. Portia still sounded like she thought this was going to be easy. Rach and I knew it was never going to be easy.

"I don't know..." Rach held back. She didn't believe Portia could help at all.

"She's good at fixing stuff, it's why she's a PA." Justin said to Rach, smiling and making a joke out of it to try to break the ice Rach had thrown on the table. Then he looked at me. "Portia hates him too, and you know I was never his fan."

"I seriously hate Mr. Rees," Portia added, giving Rach a smile. "He's a weasel. Like my dad. An arrogant asshole and a player. I hate men like that."

Rach laughed. The sound caught me by surprise as it broke like a crack of sunshine through her meds, but it was gone as fast as it came. I reached across the table and held her hand. She was not normal today. But we had a chance here, and we had to take it.

I looked at Rach when she answered, "Okay. Where should we meet?"

Maybe it was being here in New York that was affecting her moods. Maybe it was the pressure of facing the memories she kept trying to scrub out as hard as I did.

"Our place. If you like," Portia offered.

"Where are you?" I asked, as I squeezed Rach's hand, deploying the same type of reassurance Justin had. Rach and I, we were just as tight. Definitely still were. *We are...*

"In Queens."

Justin pulled out his cell and was typing something. My cell

46

buzzed in my jacket pocket. I took it out. He'd sent me the address and I guess also checked that he had the right number and I hadn't deleted him off my contacts.

I smiled at him. "Thanks." We'd been good friends when I'd worked here. Maybe I'd sold him short by cutting him off, but I'd just wanted to protect Rach and Saint by cutting all my ties with New York.

"When should we come?" Rach asked.

"We're visiting Justin's mum tonight, and I'll need time to think anyway. What about tomorrow night or Wednesday?"

"Tomorrow," I stated. The sooner the better. Every hour counted, as far as I was concerned. Every hour impacted on Rach's health and kept us away from Saint.

"Okay, at seven?"

"Okay."

Portia stood up. "We need to get back to work." She picked up her packet of barely eaten sandwiches.

Justin stood too. "We'll see you tomorrow."

"Yeah." I nodded. He lifted a fist. I bumped it. Then he opened his hand and offered it to me, I clasped it for a moment, then lastly we struck hands in a loose high five. I guess it was like a bridge over the months I hadn't replied to his texts.

"Bye," I said.

When they walked away, he gripped the back of Portia's neck gently, then leaned to whisper something in her ear.

It looked like I had had her wrong.

"Why do you think they can help?" Rach asked me in a bitter voice.

I looked at her. The full weight of the baggage that I'd carried to New York hit me in the chest. Her eyes were alight with anger. There was a bipolar storm brewing, and it was coming in from the east and about to hit me full force in a Rachel-style hurricane of emotion. "Because I don't know what else will. Maybe it'll help, maybe it won't, but it's worth seeing if it will, and don't knock it until we've tried it, honey." Fuck, I knew what was coming from the look in her eyes.

"Why did you come here in the summer? Why didn't you tell me? Why would you do that?"

Do what? Try to make sure I could adopt our son so I can get that asshole out of his life... Oh, for no real reason at all, Rach. "Let's not have that conversation here; save it for the hotel." I stood up.

She sighed when she stood. Even that slight sound had a heavy, bitter, accusing note to it. She didn't want to stall on the conversation, she was ready to fly at me. But she was going to have to wait, I wasn't having a fight in a café when I knew damn well she'd end up shouting.

We left our empty coffee cups on the table and walked out.

"Where do you want to go? Central Park or something?" I offered, hoping I could distract her and get her mood back up before we had this face-off.

"No. I want to go back to the hotel."

She wasn't going to let me stall very long, then, and probably not long enough for her temper to diffuse.

The weight pressing down on me jumped harder on my shoulders.

CHAPTER SIX

Rachel

Anger bubbled in my veins, fizzing through them. I let it play and nurtured it with words of paranoia as we walked back to the hotel.

Why had Jason done it?

Anger invaded everything and it felt good. It tingled in my nerves and fired sparks off in my belly. It felt good to have some sort of emotion. My meds were wearing off. I was escaping the bland, heavy, dark emptiness—slipping free of the chains.

I had feelings. They may be imbalanced sometimes, and irrational most of the time, but I was alive. I was. I wanted to be in charge of my life.

Jason didn't rule it.

And he'd come here in the summer without asking me, and interfered.

He'd no right.

He'd prodded Declan.

Saint wasn't even his! Saint was my son! I should get to make the decisions! Not him!

As soon as Jason shut the door of our hotel room, I said, "I would have told you not to come and see Declan if you'd've asked me." They were vicious words, but my bipolar was a vicious thing when it wanted to be. It was nasty at times and I didn't care if it was right or wrong. I was glad to have those vicious thoughts back. I'd rather that than emptiness.

49

"You weren't in a state to be asked, and one of the reasons you were so messed up was because of the pressure from Mr. Rees not completing his stuff on the paternity so we could get going with the adoption. I came here to make him do the damned DNA test to clear up any argument."

"You provoked him! And now he's changed his mind! And you lied to me!"

He sat down on the bed in a sort of collapsing motion, like he'd been pushed down, and his head dropped forward as he answered me and ran his hands through his hair. "I didn't lie. I just didn't tell you. You were ill. You didn't need to know. It would have upset you." He looked up at me when he said the last bit.

"Yeah, it sure has upset me! You shouldn't have come here and messed with him."

He didn't come back at me, and his eyes said he thought it had changed Declan's mind too. He'd regretted coming here without me.

"Was that why you didn't want me to go into the office today? So you could hide it?"

"No. I was trying to protect you. That's what I do. I try to protect you and Saint. That's what I did then, and it's what I'm doing now. I was worried about you. I came here to make things better for you."

"So you shut me out!"

"Not like that, Rach." His hands gripped his thighs, holding on, in an expression of frustration, with his jaw clenched. But then he stood suddenly, turned his back on me and walked over to the window, to look out.

We didn't argue often, because he hated arguing. He avoided it. This was what he did—turned his back on me and walked away, or went out for a run to get away.

He turned around. I waited for the words… *I'm going for a run*… Sometimes, before I'd gone on to heavy meds, and before I'd walked into the river, when my bipolar had hit a nasty mood,

I'd played with him, pushed and pushed him to see if I could make him break and get really angry and shout at me. He never had gotten really angry. That wasn't Jason. The golden fall sunshine poured through the voile curtain behind him, etching out what was so beautiful about him.

I wanted sex.

The urge flooded me with a sudden hard hunger.

I had emotions, and feelings, and life inside me again. I wanted sex.

When I breathed out I didn't say anymore, just walked over there, clasped his head with both hands and kissed him, hard.

I wanted sex.

From his hesitant response he didn't know what to make of it. But that didn't matter. He liked to avoid conflict and what better way to avoid it? I could let him avoid it and have my way.

His arms wrapped around me as he kissed me back, and then I was pushing his coat off his shoulders, and pulling his top off.

Jason got me like no one else ever had. He could take my bomb blasts of craziness and absorb and forget them just as easily as he comforted me when I was down. His eyes told me he'd taken the kiss as a peace offering. It wasn't.

He gave me a broad smile when he pulled my sweater and top off in return. He liked sex as much as I did, and the equality of our addiction shone in his eyes.

I shoved his shoulders and knocked him back against the window before he could do anymore. It pulled the curtain on the rod, but the curtain didn't tear. I dropped to my knees and undid his belt buckle.

"Rach." His fingers ran into my hair.

I didn't look up at him, just undid his button and his zipper, then pulled down his jeans and boxers with one sharp tug.

"Shit." He laughed as his back bumped against the window, then his head hit against it as he looked up. I consumed him, physically and mentally. In my head it gave me control over him.

The wicked thoughts that spun around made me suck him harder with hunger and viciousness. It was the bipolar doing this. My Mr. Hyde. The angry side of me.

I hadn't had angry sex with Jason before, and I could tell he didn't know I was still angry; he was being too gentle. His fingers stroked through my hair and he groaned in a low guttural sound of innocent pleasure.

This was the me that Declan knew.

Jason had unleashed that bitter, vindictive hard-edged woman, and he'd have to deal with her, because she was a part of me. He'd learn that this was angry sex. I wanted anger back. This was a battle. I wanted him to come in my mouth. He'd hate that. He preferred to come in me. But I wanted to be in control. Because it would make me feel better. It would just make me feel… This was me. This was how I'd had sex with loads of people. I ruled them. I managed it. I was in control.

He held my head and sighed out as I sucked the length of him hard, with my fist gripping him tight, so he'd feel completely absorbed and handled. I flicked my tongue and nipped his sensitive tip, being mean, really, not sexy.

He groaned louder, maybe with pain, but maybe still with pleasure, and his fingertips pressed hard into my scalp. He was enjoying this. I didn't know that I wanted him to. A part of me wanted him to hate it. I needed him to hate it. I didn't want him to like this me.

Declan had enjoyed my angry sex. He used to make me mad at him just so I'd be angry when we did it, he'd give me drugs and then do something that would annoy me, and then there would be a battle, with him and his friends.

I gripped Jason's backside, urging him to move, to press into me, to be aggressive and angry back. That was what I wanted—a fight. A sex fight.

I suppose, with Declan, it had really been rape. Only I'd been too confused, mentally sick and misguided to ever bother to say no to him. I hadn't known how to say no to guys. Jason had taught me that.

Jason started pressing into my mouth, but not fighting.

Jason didn't do that. He wasn't Declan, or any of the other bad guys I'd punished and tortured myself with.

Jason's fingers stroked through my hair. The gentleness of the movement touched something inside me. The sounds in his throat were definitely sounds of pleasure and appreciation—gratitude. Not anger. He sighed out hard when I let him withdraw, with a guttural sound of satisfaction.

"If you don't want me to come, you'd better stop," he said a moment later, in such a sweet, Jason-like voice. His pitch said I love you, and I love making love to you but I want you to get something out of this.

I still wanted him to come. I wanted to win. To prove to myself that I could still win—but it didn't feel like a fight anymore, just a competition.

"Rach. Shit." He clasped at my head and pushed into my mouth. Then he came, throbbing in my hand and hot and bitter in my throat. I held his buttocks and swallowed, then he was pulling me up by his grip in my hair.

"I love you." The words were said over my lips, then his mouth came down on mine. Whatever he'd thought about my sudden, random decision to suck him off, he'd enjoyed it and he was not complaining. He loved absorbing my bomb-blasts of madness.

His hands cradled the back of my thighs, then clutched and lifted me. He walked forward and threw me on to my back on the bed, with a growl that was half laugh.

"Ah!" I squealed. He was killing my bad mood as swiftly as I'd attacked him. His hands went to the waistband of my jeans and undid the button, then he pulled my jeans, and the thong he'd chosen this morning, down to my thighs.

He hadn't taken his pants off, and he didn't take my bra off but dived straight into reciprocating with oral sex.

His tongue touched me as his fingers still gripped my jeans. I rocked my hips up against him, my fingers splayed over his hair, urging him on, smiling up at the ceiling. I wanted to come. I wanted to escape. I wanted more sensations and feelings.

Give me every sensation and feeling, let me fly.

He slipped his fingers into me, and moved them fast, in and out, over and over. Like he wanted me to come quick. He was applying the same intensity I'd used on him. That was all he'd seen my aggressive sex as, intensity.

I fell into an orgasm with a wonderful rush I hadn't known for months. *Yes...* I wanted to scream. I'd broken the chains of my meds. Escaped them. I could feel!

He rose over me, his erection protruding and ready. He'd have pulled my jeans off but I rolled on to my belly. I was enjoying our half-naked sex. Obeying my implied order, he yanked me up on to all-fours and shoved into me, doggy-style. My fingers clasped the bed covers as he worked.

When he bumped against me, we bumped the headboard against the wall. He clasped my shoulders to pull me back into him and stop the bed rocking. It intensified my feeling but it didn't stop the bed moving. I pushed back against him, fighting again. To ruin it for him, to make him come first. But it was only to make the sex better, not for a vicious reason. It wasn't bipolar doing it, it was me.

The air in the room filled up with the sound of us having sex, panting, sighs, and little catches of throaty sounds as the bed creaked along with his rhythm, in a symphony for the fun of anyone in the room next to ours.

"Come first!" I shouted, when he hadn't broken. I was getting close to the edge, the sensation in my blood was so sweet, but there was still a need for competition, for me to win.

"No way."

His hand came around the front of my thigh and pressed on to the sensitive spot at the front of my sex. I came. I couldn't help it. I didn't want to… It was a beautiful sensation. "Ahh!" I cried out, slightly angry and slightly celebrating.

He thrust about six more times. The intensified sensation of it made me wish I'd given in and come earlier. He came then, pressing deep into me and holding still.

Then he leaned down and growled by my ear.

I laughed and when he withdrew I tumbled to my back smiling. My jeans were halfway down my thighs but my bra was still on.

He knelt back, his buttocks on his heels, his chest bare and his jeans open and hanging down. The sight made me laugh again.

He poked his forefinger into my belly. "What was that about? Why are you laughing?"

I laughed again. Perhaps it sounded a little twisted. I wasn't even sure why I was laughing. I smiled, though, my anger forgotten.

Why had I been angry? I couldn't even really remember.

He leaned down and kissed a scar left by a stretch mark on my belly. Then he tumbled on to his back.

Jason was not like any other guy I'd been with. He was nice, it was in the heart of him, bred into him by his nice parents. He couldn't be bad or mean to me. Even when I'd walked into a river and nearly drowned Saint. Even when I was angry and was used to beating myself up by winding up bad guys who'd treat me badly… Jason wouldn't be wound up. He'd never lash out or hit me, he'd never even be violent when we had sex. Violence and aggression weren't in Jason.

He was the thing that made me different. Made me good—like him.

I laughed.

"Rach…" He rolled on to his side and his fingers brushed down the side of my face. "Are you still mad at me?"

I sighed. "Yes, and no."

55

His lips twisted a little sideways. "What does that mean? Are we okay then?"

"Yes and no."

He smiled fully. "I'm saying yes for you, then. We're okay."

"We are," I answered. But the words cut through me and my smile fell. The images of my bad behavior before I'd met Jason were in my head. But they reminded me. "I want to go to the club I used to go to, where I met Declan, and see if he's there? May we go tonight? If you want to find out facts we can trip him up with, you'll find them there, not at his office or from that woman, and I want to see him. I want to stand up to him. I want him to know I'm going to fight."

His lips twisted, like he was trying to work out the puzzles inside me. He never would. I never had. Bipolar was an unbreakable code, a maze you could get lost in over and over again, with dead ends and wrong turns.

"We'll go to the club if you want. But we'll speak to Portia and Justin too. I had my doubts about Portia before we left New York, but I used to get along with Justin and I trust him, so I trust her."

His fingers ran along my jawline, gently.

I looked into his brown eyes. "I was really angry at you—"

"I know. I didn't miss what was going on, Rach."

"But I was having angry sex with you and you didn't play."

He laughed at me.

I smacked his arm. "Don't laugh at me!"

"Honey, you having sex with me is never going to make me angry." He held my gaze, just looking into my eyes. Just being Jason. Challenging me with silence louder than anyone else had challenged me by shouting.

When he looked at me like that he'd always made me feel like he saw me—the real me—the emotionally naked woman—and he didn't judge her. That girl who'd run away from abuse at the age of fifteen into a relationship that had only ever been consensual abuse, and that was how it had gone on. I'd let men abuse me constantly and not cared... because I'd never cared about myself until I'd met Jason. I'd learned to care about me because he cared about me.

Why had I been angry at him? I couldn't remember. I knew why I'd wanted sex with him, though.

"I think I used to use sex as medication..." Of course then I had been too ill to even know I was ill and it was that which had been firing it. But now that I thought about it, I'd used it to keep my mood up, or fight my lows, because when I'd been having sex, even if it was letting someone abuse me, I'd felt something. I'd connected with the world—with the one emotion I could understand, that made me feel good. "I feel better now." The sex we'd had, had changed my mood.

I'd used sex because I'd always felt better after sex, no matter who it was with, where or how—until I'd finally realized it was a form of self-harming, and what I did was twisted out of shape. Then I'd run away to end it all, to escape who I'd become.

Then Jason had found me—or I'd found him.

He'd been a knight in shining armor to my damsel in distress, and like a fairytale we'd married and run off to Oregon for our happy ending.

But the problem with fairytales was that they ended at the beginning. The couples begin their lives together when the fairytale ends—fairytales never say what happened next.

Jason and I were living what happened next, and what happened next wasn't always good, or happy—sometimes stuff went wrong and forever didn't happen. That thought sent fear sliding into my veins.

He leaned down and pressed a kiss on my lips, maybe seeing the mood shift in my eyes. Then he rolled on to his back. "Shall we watch a movie then eat at Joe's? Then we'll be brave and go to this club of yours, if you want? And you can have your moment to tell Mr. Rees what a jerk-off he is."

"Yeah." I rolled over and pillowed my head on his chest. His arm came around me.

He made me feel safe.

"*I was trying to protect you. That's what I do. I try to protect you and Saint...*" Yeah. That's what he did, and it was one of the reasons I loved him so much. He'd been protecting me from the day I'd met him, when he hadn't even known who I was or what I was like.

Watching a movie included stripping right off and making love again, slowly, the opposite of the way I'd prodded him to do it before, making it clear, although I didn't think it was deliberate, how different it was being with a nice guy who loved me. He didn't just protect me, he cherished me, and when he touched my body everything about it said that was true.

He couldn't know the difference, though—between sex to have an orgasm and sex with someone who loved you—because he'd never done it with anyone he didn't care about or who didn't care about him.

That thought hung around in my head as we dressed to go out.

I'd dressed up for the club so I felt overdressed in the restaurant in my high heels, tight skirt, and glittery top. Jason looked fine, he never did over-dressed. He had a dark shirt on that I'd gotten him last Christmas and his black skinny pants.

But then, as we waited in the cold, in the queue to the club, I started to panic. He wouldn't fit in here. It wasn't about what he wore. It was him. I'd never met a good guy in here. He was too nice for this place. Declan would eat him alive in this place.

Jason was gonna be shocked.

He'd see who I'd been.

He'd understand who he'd gotten together with.

He'd never done anything wild in his life until he'd met me. I'd told him everything from the get-go, but he hadn't lived like

58

I had so he couldn't understand or visualize it when I'd talked about it.

I was mad taking him here…

Why had I said I'd take him here?

What if he got hurt? What if he didn't like what he saw?

I wanted to turn around and run. I didn't want to see Declan anymore. But then Jason would wanna know why I'd changed my mind. Every muscle in my body tightened as concern flared into anxiety, and it tightened about my lungs, restricting my breath.

"Two," Jason said when we got to the door.

I turned my head into his shoulder.

I'd had sex with every one of the security guys who worked at the club. I didn't want to face them, and I didn't want to face that me either—the old self-abusing me. Not in front of Jason. So why had I said I wanted to try and find Declan here?

"Go on." The guy unclipped the rope.

Jason's arm hung around my shoulders as we walked past. I kept my head turned and tried not to remember the things I wished I'd never done. I wished the past could be scrubbed out, scratched out—burnt.

This place was an evil nightmare.

Why had I asked to come?

The walls closed in as we walked up the stairs, and I actually saw a couple of hands reaching out from them. My heart pounded hard. I was seeing things…

Jason's arm fell from my shoulders. Instead, he gripped my hand and pulled me on up the stairs. We checked our coats at the cloakroom; my hands shook when I handed mine over.

"Are you cold?" Jason asked me.

I shook my head.

When we walked into the club the noise and the beat of the music bounced through my chest, reverberating in my bones. I loved music. I loved noise. It pulled me back from the anxiety threatening to drown me. I wanted to dance. I could forget about Declan if I danced. But we weren't here to dance.

Why hadn't my brain thought harder about this?

But we were here now and if I was gonna face Declan we needed to get into what I used to call the dirty millionaires' den—the VIP area. That was why I'd slept with the security men because for sex they'd let me in there to mix with the rich and famous. The guys who kept themselves fit and had money.

I'd walked out on the money too when I'd run away from Declan; he'd given me loads of meaningless trinkets to pay me off for the things I'd done with him. I hadn't wanted any of them. I'd left them all at his apartment.

"So where do we go now?" Jason shouted into my ear over the music, as his arm wrapped around me and his hand touched my waist.

"We get a drink and then we go up to the VIP bar, where Declan hangs out!" And I'd look at my past and probably see it as it really was for the first time. I didn't want to go up there anymore. I wanted to be like Jason and run away.

He took my hand and wove us a path through the crowded club, holding on to my hand behind his hip as we walked single file.

When we got to the bar, he turned. "What do you want?"

"You!"

He smiled. "To drink!"

"Vodka and orange juice!"

"With your meds!"

"One won't harm!"

"Okay. One! I'll let you charge yourself up so you can face him!" He turned to order.

I'd guess he'd been thinking all the way here about the moment we'd face Declan.

My heart pounded out along with the dance track that was playing. The music had a really heavy bass beat that was getting into my blood. I wanted to be up close to Jason, dancing and not thinking about Declan, with my arms on Jason's shoulders and my hips rocking against his.

Jason turned around, holding a narrow glass containing my vodka and orange, and a large glass of lager for him. I took my glass.

"Do you still wanna do this? You don't have to."

Jason's instinct to protect was precious. I wanted to give in to it and back out. Everything in me screamed to back out. But I couldn't let myself, because if Declan was upstairs, I needed to tell him I wasn't going to let him win; to push the demons of the past out of the way; to make him stop.

Jason's hand settled on my shoulder, sheltering me, as I turned towards the stairs at the side of the room. My heart played a beat right along with the heavy bass of the music.

I didn't recognize the guy who stood before the rope.

I glanced up into the air. *Thank you, good, sweet Lord.* That was one nightmare I did not have to face.

But the guy had to let us up to the VIP area otherwise there was zero point in us being here and if he didn't know me…

"Hi!" I shouted over the music. "We're friends of Declan Rees. I come here with him all the time." I hoped the guy was so new he wouldn't know it was a lie. I wanted to add, is he upstairs? But if I asked, then it would make it sound more like I didn't know him.

"Do you?" The guy looked at Jason with disbelieving eyes, judging his shirt and his shoes. Jason wasn't dressed like he hung out with VIPs.

I lifted to my toes and said into the guy's ear, "If you want to take the risk of not letting us in and have Declan rip your balls off and get you sacked, go ahead take the risk…"

It turned out threatening worked with new guys. He unclipped the rope and let us through. I glanced back at Jason when we climbed the stairs, feeling like I'd gotten away with a great victory.

Suddenly I was invincible, made of iron and sparkling with gold, and my mood bubbled up in an effervescent fizz, bursting out into a smile and a weird laugh. I didn't care if Declan was at the top of the stairs. I was going to win, and I was going to make him feel as small as a flea on the back of a cat when I told him what I thought of him, and his mean nature.

"What?" Jason asked. Jason's hand settled on my hip as we reached the top of the stairs and turned to face the blue room with its plush blue-velvet furnishings.

I'd had sex in this room, many times. With more than one person. I looked at Jason, refusing the stuff filling my head. "Nothing." Just memories. Just the images my broken brain sent me, like I wanted to see my embarrassing, shitty history. I didn't want to have ever been that person and so I told myself I hadn't been. I was who I was now; with Jason. An angel of vengeance, burning bright, alight with fire.

Thoughts raced around, bouncing off the edges of my skull. Images from the past mainly. Memories that should revolt me, but they didn't now that my mood was soaring high. I'd been a sick person and Jason didn't realize how sick. I was different with him.

My gaze leapt about the room, looking everywhere. I couldn't see Declan. He wasn't here. Now I wanted more than anything for him to be here. But it was a quiet Monday night, there were no famous people in the bar either, and no one I knew.

Jason found a free table and sat down. I sat next to him.

When he leaned forward to put his drink down, his hand rested on my thigh.

Lust danced up my nerves and clasped in my belly. It hadn't been a sexual touch. It had been a reassuring touch—but I was high.

I wanted sex.

"So what do we do now that we're here and he isn't?" he said.

I knew what I wanted to do, but I didn't tell him.

He smiled. "Well, I guess we'll work it out. What did you do when you came here with him?"

I took a breath. If he was going to understand and know enough to gather some dirt on Declan, then I had to be honest. "Had sex and took cocaine."

Jason's eyes widened. "Rach…"

There he was, saying a load of words with silence. After the first time he and I had had sex he'd told me I should have more respect for myself. His words had stayed with me—now he said the same again with his eyes. He knew I hadn't respected myself until I'd met him.

He'd always respected me.

"That was what we did. You asked; I told you. I'm only telling you the truth. You need to know it if we're gonna find something to trap him."

He sighed out a breath and lifted his arm. But I didn't want a cuddle; I wasn't in the mood for a cuddle. I wanted sex. I put my drink down, then climbed on to his lap, straddling his hips. We'd gotten together in a club and kissed in this position, getting carried away, but he'd balked at the idea of doing it in the club. I wanted to do it in a club.

"Rach." Jason's palms settled on my thighs. "What are you doing?"

"Kissing you." I lifted his face and lowered my head until our lips met. He answered my kiss, but it was reserved.

I pressed my tongue into his mouth, and his moved around mine, but not really participating, just responding, as his hands remained on my thighs, unmoving. The need for sex roared in me. I was a lioness on the hunt. If I did it with him here it would wash away every other memory; it would cleanse me. I had a belief, with a blinding clarity, that sex with Jason in this club was the answer to everything.

In my messed-up head it made everything fall into place. All we had to do was do it here and everything would be alright.

I rocked over his crotch, trying to arouse him.

His hold on my thighs firmed and he broke the kiss. "Stop."

My hands clasped either side of his head and I stared into his eyes. "I want to have sex with you, in here."

"It's not even busy, people are watching."

People had watched when I'd done it with others, Declan had been one of them; that was how I'd met him. And when we'd been together he used to play games like challenging me to see how many people in here would have sex with me in one night.

"Please…" I begged Jason. I wanted to forget. "I want sex. I need it."

CHAPTER SEVEN

Jason

Shit, I shouldn't be letting her try to turn me on here…

But this was what I'd missed about Rach. The edginess. The way she made my heart race, daring me to do the things I'd never done, or even thought about. I loved her, and it was this side of her I'd fallen for, and it was so long since she'd felt free enough to be this person. She'd been up and down today, but she'd been happy for moments, and she was on the steps of happiness now. I didn't want to take that away from her. I didn't want to lose it again…

Fuck what I should and shouldn't do!

She wanted this and I wanted her.

I wanted to be with her in the way we'd been the night we'd first gotten together, and let friendship twist into what had become the best thing I'd ever known.

I wanted life to be at its best again.

"Wheelchair restroom. You go first," I whispered into her ear.

She rocked back and laughed. It had been months since I'd heard her laugh like that, and maybe it was still a key or two off normal, but it was proper laughter.

With a huge smile, the biggest I'd seen on her face since before the river thing, she climbed off my lap, turned around, and walked away. I watched her and leaned forward to pick up my lager. Rach moved in a way that spoke of sex. Her whole body said sex. I sipped from my glass. Even since having Saint she'd kept the figure of a model, and her blonde, straight hair slipped across her shoulders.

After about two minutes I put down my lager and followed; my blood pulsed and my hard-on formed while I walked. I pushed the door open, went inside, shut it, and locked it.

Rach was leaning against the white sink. She pulled up her skirt.

Lust growled inside me with a surge of reckless desire. I crossed the room, unbuckling my belt as I walked.

It was a toss-up whether this, or having sex in the alley with her—the first time we'd done it—was the craziest thing I'd ever done. But I liked that she made me do crazy stuff, it made our lives exciting. It was the thing that had made me come alive. The adrenalin that made my blood pound through my arteries was all love for Rach.

Within moments I'd pulled her skirt all the way up, disposed of her panties, and was inside her again for the third time today, pumping hard, because this just had to be quick. Her fingers clasped my shoulders through my shirt as she balanced on the sink, then they fell to my biceps as I gripped her ass and took her with a rough thirst. We'd stopped having proper sex after the incident in the summer, she'd been too doped up on her meds, but a week ago I'd pushed her boundaries because I missed exciting, heart-pounding sex, and now within just over a week we were doing this…

Her hand came up and ran over my hair when she came and cried out with a breathy sound of exhilaration, making way too much noise, but the music still pounded outside the door.

Her body called for me to come, massaging me with a tight spasm as the warm fluid of her orgasm flooded around me. I went over the edge into an orgasm that had me weak-kneed and shaking, it was so deep. My forehead dropped on to her shoulder as I breathed, getting control of myself again.

"I love you," I said into her ear when I lifted my head.

"I love you too."

I withdrew and tidied myself up while she peed and sorted herself out. Then she flushed the toilet, smiled over her shoulder at me, unlocked the door, and walked out. I locked it again and caught the image of myself in the mirror.

Shit.

Guilt cut through me.

"Shit!" I said it aloud.

I shouldn't have let her do that. It was her bipolar that had worked her up into a desire for naughty sex, not Rach herself, and now she'd think that's what I wanted—her to be at the sick level of crazy.

Fuck. I slapped a palm over the reflection of my face in the mirror, then turned to take a piss, to delay going back out there.

I loved her effervescent, addictive, and infectious nature, it was what I wanted, but not at the cost of her sanity, and this wasn't the Rach I'd met, not really. I'd met the down Rach first and then I'd discovered her rollercoaster, but she hadn't been ill like she'd bee this summer. She was still really sick.

On Halloween she'd talked about wanting to find herself again, and I'd admitted that I'd missed the woman who hadn't been doped up on medication. Shit. I hoped she hadn't taken that to heart.

I had my suspicions now. And I didn't want her to make herself sicker... Or degrade herself because she was ill and lacking judgment. That wasn't what I wanted. There must be something in the middle. Some drugs she could be on to feel better, that wouldn't wreck her life.

I loved her highs, but I loved all of her, everything about her. I just wanted her to be well.

When I went out she was at the bar buying another drink for herself. I still had half a lager on the table.

She leaned over, talking to the barman. The move and the

pose reminded me of when I'd seen her serving people when she was a waitress. She used to use her body to get better tips, by leaning over too far. The bartender was looking down the front of her top.

I didn't go over there. If I went over there I might do something stupid. Like drag him over the bar and pound him to death with my fists.

The glass she came back with had orange juice in it. When she put it down I picked it up and sipped it. It had vodka in it too. She wasn't meant to be drinking with her meds. I put it down but didn't say anything. She knew that I knew it was there.

She twisted around and leaned forward to speak into my ear so she didn't have to shout over the music. "The guy said Declan still comes in here."

I nodded. My brain wasn't really on Mr. Rees right now; it needed a moment to get back into gear.

"He still does cocaine, but the guy said there's none available in the club."

My hand slid into her hair, holding her close as I leaned to her ear. "How do you know?"

"I asked him if I could get any. He said, no, so I told him I knew Declan, and I knew Declan took it here with other people. After that he said, yeah, but he doesn't get it in here."

"Did you ever see him buying it? If we could get him on a drug charge that would blow up his case."

"I know, but I never saw him buy it. He used to buy a lot for parties, though."

Well, that was our answer then; we needed to work out where he was buying his drugs and get the cops to catch him doing it.

When I woke up the voile curtain was drawn back, so I could see the Brooklyn skyline clearly. The sky was a pale pink. Dawn was breaking but the sun hadn't risen over the tops of the buildings yet. I was lying on my belly, gripping the pillow, I didn't move, just looked at Rach, who was also gilded by the dawn.

She was standing at the edge of the window, watching the sun rise, her arms folded over her chest.

She appeared wide awake, as if she'd been standing there for hours.

I rolled to my side. "Rach. How long have you been up?"

She glanced sideways at me and smiled. "Ages. Most of the night."

I was certain now. The suspicion I'd had last night was right. I was sure of it. "Do you want to go for a run?"

She nodded.

It would help distract her mind.

When she went into the bathroom I wanted to call Mom, but it was too early, it would have to wait until we came back.

We ran down to Prospect Park again, our heavy breaths misting in the cold morning air. It was quiet because it was early and a different atmosphere hung in the air. When I'd lived in New York I'd run in the evenings, it was rare that I'd gone for an early run, but I wished I'd done it more often. I preferred the quieter streets.

When we got back to the hotel, Rach went into the bathroom for a shower, throwing a look at me that offered sex. My heart pumped harder. "I'll be in there in a minute."

I picked up my cell from the nightstand and looked up my contacts, waited until the toilet flushed and the shower turned on, then I pressed the call icon and walked over to the window away from the bathroom.

"Hello, Jason. How are you, honey?"

"Mom, would you do me a favor, but you need to be quick?"

"What, sweetheart?"

"Go and look in mine and Rach's room."

"Okay, did you forget something?"

I could hear her walking. "I think Rachel didn't bring her meds, but she hasn't said. Would you just see if they're in one of the drawers by the bed?" The door creaked.

"Okay. Wait a minute."

She was quiet for a moment, then she said, "They're here."

Fuck. "Okay, thanks for looking."

"Do you want me to mail them to you?"

"I don't know. Yeah. I guess. But we're seeing a specialist here next week."

"I'll send them so they'll reach you tomorrow."

"Thanks. I better go, Rach is in the shower. How's Saint?"

"Sleeping, with a full belly."

"Thanks for everything you're doing, Mom."

"You're welcome."

I ended the call, probably a bit too quickly because I was worried about Rach wondering where I was. I left my cell on the nightstand and stripped off. My hands shook as guilt took a knife to my chest over last night at the club.

I was walking a high wire with Rachel and I didn't know how to stay on it. What was a right step and what was a wrong one? How did I stay on the wire with her? I was afraid I'd fall off, and there was too much weight trying to push me off.

When I got into the shower, she turned to me. Her wet hair was stuck to her scalp, her shoulders, and her breasts, as the water poured over her. Her fingers came up to the back of my head and pulled me down for a kiss.

When I made love to her up against the tiles, it was not with lust or with excitement because she was being naughty and challenging me, or because she was playing games with me burning out her mood—high or low—but because I loved her. I was just making love to her.

I watched her when she dressed afterward. Wondering whether to say anything, but I didn't know what to say, so I didn't speak.

I wanted to protect her, but what could I do to help her if she didn't want to help herself?

When we were clothed she looked at me. "Where do you wanna go?"

"To get something to eat, I'm starving."

"Then we can go over to Declan's apartment and I can see if he's there. I'll ask the security guards for some clues if he isn't."

"If you want to." I'd come here to fight. But all I could think about when she mentioned Mr. Rees and talking to the security guys was that barman last night. I didn't want fighting to mean her using her body to get attention.

I knew who she'd been before, what she'd done. I didn't care about it. She'd never been like that since she'd been with me, and I didn't want her to ever have to be like that again.

I stuck close to her as she asked after Mr. Rees in the condos' reception area, and when they said he wasn't in, I stayed even closer when she spoke to the security guys. We didn't get any clues from them.

CHAPTER EIGHT

Rachel

Jason's friends lived in a line of cute, three-story, homey-looking buildings that were surrounded by white-painted cast-iron railings. Each floor was a condo, and on the second floor was a white-railed balcony. Jason's friends were in a ground-floor condo.

It was the woman, Portia, who opened the door. "Hello. I hope you're expecting to eat, we made dinner."

We hadn't been. My plan with Jason had been to get in and out quickly and eat after, but it looked like that plan wasn't gonna work out. Not having eaten was gonna be our excuse to leave early.

"Come on in. This way." She turned around and led us into a sunny hall, then opened a door on the right-hand side and walked into a living room that was equally sunny.

"This is a nice place," I said, as I saw through the glass doors at the back. They had a small backyard out there.

"The place I was in before was up in an attic, so it's a contrast, but we like it here, especially because we have the garden."

I could understand why Declan had employed her as his assistant. It would look good on him to have her preppy, British voice answering his phone and calling his business contacts.

"Jason." Jason's black friend walked out of another door into the room; I guess he'd come out of their kitchen. I peered around the door jamb; it looked like he'd been laying out the table that was in there. This wasn't a big place, but it was about triple the size of the apartment Jason had been in when I'd met him, and it was theirs. We hadn't gotten our own place. We'd been planning it, but since I'd walked into the river, Jason had stopped mentioning it and he was the only one working now, so I couldn't raise a deposit or feel like I could suggest the idea. It would be telling him how to spend his money.

I looked at Jason's friend and held out my hand. "Hi. It's nice to see you." I couldn't remember his name. That was the only reason I said it.

"Yeah, thanks for asking us over, Justin." Jason looked from the guy to his girlfriend. "Portia."

"Justin." Now that I knew his name I offered my hand again. "Hi." The first time looked less odd now.

"Hi." He shook my hand, then fist-bumped with Jason.

I looked at Portia, trying to remember who I was back in Oregon, the person Jason's family had learned to like; if I wanted these people to like me I needed to be her. "Can I help in the kitchen?"

It was much easier to be me in Oregon, wrapped up in the love of Jason's family. I was all twisted out of shape here.

"We're just serving up; you could give me a hand if you like."

She'd made a tomato and pasta dish, with salad, there was nothing fancy about it, and she talked casually to me as we put everything on to the table.

She was so different from me. She was the sort of girl I would have pictured Jason with if he'd been a stranger I'd been watching in a bar.

But she was easy to talk to once I'd relaxed and by the time we'd finished dinner Jason was laughing with his friend, and I felt at ease. I liked them.

We sat down in the living room when we'd finished eating, the boys gripping beer bottles and Portia and I sitting opposite each other.

I'd been watching the way she and Justin communicated. They were friends as well as lovers. They talked and told us stories, butting in on each other and they laughed and glanced at each other all the time.

I looked at Jason. Had we ever been like that? He was talking to Justin, sitting back in an armchair, his beer bottle moving and lifting, emphasizing the words of his conversation. But he wasn't relaxed. There was a tension around his lips, and it was like he had a slight frown. I bet if I touched his shoulders, the muscle there would be solid.

He glanced at me, as though he sensed me watching him, and smiled. There were the words in the silence. *Are you okay?*

The muscle in my belly tightened when I nodded. He wasn't relaxed with me. I couldn't remember when he'd been relaxed around me. But he must have been in the beginning. At least when we'd been alone…

When Jason looked back at Justin and they carried on talking, Portia sat forward in her chair

"So how do you think I can help you?"

I looked at her. "Jason wants to trap Declan. The only idea he has to do it is to find out where and when Declan buys his drugs. Then we'll get the police to catch him at it. He wouldn't win custody with a police record for buying drugs. We went to the club he goes to, but the barman was sure people didn't buy drugs there, and I asked the security guys in the condos where he lives, but they wouldn't say anything."

"I didn't even know he took drugs 'til you said. So I doubt he'd put a contact like that through me and maybe he's stopped taking cocaine while his wife is suing for divorce. I've typed a lot of letters about the divorce and his lawyer is always calling, either about your case or the divorce. So maybe he's being careful. If he was caught buying cocaine it would damage his divorce case too and his access to his other kids."

Shit. I had an idea. "Jason." He looked over. "I could threaten

74

him. We don't need any more evidence. I know what he does." I hadn't even thought about the power I had. I had a lot of power over Declan. I knew everything. All his dirty little secrets. Every vivid damning, fucking detail of the sleazy life he led behind his image of a respectable businessman. I had that sudden sense of being on fire. An angel in white on fire. "If I told his wife's lawyer, he'd lose access to his other kids and it would trash his settlement in his divorce. He'd give anything away to avoid that." Including Saint.

Jason's lips closed and twisted sideways. He didn't like the idea.

I looked at Portia. "Do you think that would stop him from fighting me?"

"You know him better than I do, all I know is he's a cold-hearted cheat, but he's not happy about his wife suing him—"

"Because his money came from his wife. If she leaves him he'll be hemorrhaging money," Jason said.

"His distress over his divorce has nothing to do with the love of his kids," Justin added.

"Or his wife, pretty obviously," Jason finished.

This was a hate-Declan club; sticking pins in him like we had a voodoo doll. I laughed. Probably for too long, and probably in a weird cackle. Jason looked at me. I swallowed the laughter. Maybe it hadn't even been a laughing moment.

"So what now?" Portia said.

"I'll go and talk to him again," Jason said, then took a swig from his beer bottle.

"But this time I'm coming in too." I'd wanted to face him in the club. The desire to face him revved up. I needed to face him. For Saint if not for me. But it was for me too. My righteous angel rose up, wings and arms wide, ready for revenge.

Jason choked trying to swallow his mouthful of beer, then he wiped his mouth and looked at me. "No."

It wasn't his choice. "You can't make the threat. It has to be

75

me. He'll only believe I'll do it if it's me who says it. You don't even really know what you're threatening him with."

It was like I'd punched him in the belly. He went silent and looked down at the neck of his beer, then took another swig like he was trying to distract me from his response. He only wanted to protect me, but...

"It has to be me," I said again.

"I was trying to protect you. That's what I do. I try to protect you and Saint..." I breathed in hard, holding in all the odd emotions warring in me.

After he'd swallowed his mouthful he glanced over at me again. "Whatever you want." His words were stiff and sharp and his posture had changed. I might think his protection a precious thing... But what did he think? My broken brain rarely remembered to think about him. But I'd been trapped inside myself for months. Locked in by my meds.

Justin looked at him, then me, then Portia.

Portia stood up. "Mr. Rees is in the office tomorrow. He's got a meeting at two. Do you want another glass of lemonade?" It was like they thought something wasn't right between me and Jason.

Was something not right?

I looked at Portia. "Yeah, thanks." I hadn't thought tonight would help us. I'd been wrong. I looked back at Jason. He was looking down at the beer bottle in his hand, thinking, while Justin said something else.

Was something not right? I'd always thought we were good together.

When Portia came back in, the conversation turned away from Declan, and we just talked, about anything. I liked it. I liked talking to them. They were nice people. Like Jason.

When we left their place, I was excited and on a high, buzzing with energy. It felt so good. Everything was going to work out. I was convinced. I wasn't even worried anymore. It was an absolute belief. Because I was on a high and invincible. This was what I'd given up my meds to feel. I was happy and riding it like a surfer on a wave. It was too long since I'd felt this pulsing energy and excitement.

I turned to Jason when we walked along the sidewalk heading for the subway. "Can we go to a club? I wanna dance."

We didn't go out to clubs in Oregon, we lived a small-town life. There were only a few quiet bars in his town. I wanted noise and crowds, I wanted the energy of people and music.

He stopped walking and looked at me, his arm had been around my waist, keeping me warmer, it lifted to my shoulders when he turned to face me. "Don't you want to call Mom? It's getting late to speak to Saint."

"I'll do it now." I looked down and dug my cell out of my purse. It was already too late, really, it was nearly ten. His arm fell away when I caught a fingertip of my glove in my teeth and pulled my glove off, then I crammed that into my pocket, slid up my contacts and pressed Mom's call icon. "Hey, Mom."

"Hi, Rachel. How are you?"

"Really good, thanks. Is Saint still awake? Sorry it's late."

"No, he's in bed, dear."

"Would you take the cell upstairs and put it to his mouth so I can hear him breathing, I love listening to him breathing when he's asleep."

I could tell from her breaths she'd started walking upstairs. "How are you and Grampy? I hope Saint's not wearing you out."

"No, we're fine, dear. Here you are, I'll put the cell to his mouth now." Her last words were whispered.

I could hear him breathing. It was like a soft little whisper. Before I'd gone back on the meds, on the nights I couldn't sleep because I was high, I used to lay in bed for hours listening to his little breaths. My body had made him. That little person.

"Do you feel better?" Mom asked when she came back on.

I hadn't been feeling bad. I wouldn't have even called if Jason hadn't reminded me it was getting late. Guilt jabbed a finger in my ribs. "Okay. Thanks. Do you wanna speak to Jason?"

"Not unless he has anything special to say."

I looked at him. "Do you wanna talk?"

He shook his head.

"No, he doesn't. Bye."

"Goodnight, Rachel."

When the call went dead, I stood still for a minute holding my cell, filled with memories of lying in the dark, listening to Saint breathe.

"You okay?" Jason's gloved fingers brushed my hair back behind my ear.

"Yeah."

He'd been different all day. He'd started smiling properly yesterday, but he'd stopped again today. I remembered his stiff posture at Justin and Portia's "You?" I couldn't remember the last time I'd asked him that question.

"I'm okay if you are," he answered with a twisted closed-lipped smile. "Do you still want to go dancing?"

If you are...

The thought of dancing flooded my consciousness, over the top of any thoughts of Saint—and I forgot our conversation. "Yeah."

"Then let's go dancing."

His arm wrapped around me again as I pulled my glove back on.

We went to the club we'd gone to together when I'd stayed with him in New York. It played mainly R&B music and we spent hours dancing all up close, sweaty and personal. My hands gripped his butt or the back of his neck as we swayed, ground against each other and rocked to the rhythm of the music. I was breathless and fired up with energy when we left there, and in need of sex, again. I was starving for it. I'd been through a desert over the last few months and was walking out the other side, my throat dry and my belly hungry.

We did have sex but it was in the bed, like good kids, only I went on top and rode him, pushing hard for a quick orgasm so I could enjoy the rest even more.

When we'd finished, while Jason fell asleep, I lay on my side looking out at the lights of the city which pierced through the thin curtains. I'd had a great time today, and last night. I was really enjoying being back in New York.

But what about Saint? The thought slipped through my head, it was like another part of my mind spoke to me, reminding me that things were different. How could I be happy without Saint?

I shouldn't be happy.

The thought sent me crashing down a rabbit hole like Alice in Wonderland, falling into the dark, into a pit of despair. The bad mood I tumbled into became a heavy weight pushing me down into the bed.

When I started crying Jason woke up and wrapped his arm around me, but he didn't say a thing. If he had I couldn't have found any words to answer anyway, even if I'd wanted to talk. He probably knew.

I cried myself to sleep as he reassured and comforted me. With an arm that was stiff and tight, like rock—protecting me.

CHAPTER NINE

Jason

Rach was asleep, but tonight I couldn't sleep. I sat on the floor, naked, with my back against the wall, and my arms on my bent-up knees. I didn't know what to do. I didn't know how to help her. Or how to help me.

I didn't like her being on meds any more than she liked it. But when this was the alternative... She'd been all over the place for two days. Up then down. Wild, laughing then crying.

And we weren't having loads of sex because she loved me, or even because she loved sex with me, or sex in general. Her desire for sex wasn't about me, or her. It was a bipolar-centered addiction; she didn't have any control over it when she was off meds.

How could I happily ride her rollercoaster of edgy when really it was her being sick? I didn't want her to feel sick.

I hated myself. Guilt had been lancing through my chest ever since we'd done it in that restroom last night. Then I'd kept thinking about what she must have done with other people in that club. I'd always known about her past. But... Now I could visualize it.

I didn't want to, but images kept on shoving their way into my mind.

I'd never cared about her past, or judged her on it. Since we'd been together there'd only been me. I knew that. But...

What about the future?

If she stayed off meds and she was like this… What would she do? Would she go back to making dumb decisions? Would she end up doing herself some harm, like she nearly had with Saint? All my family had been cautious around her since she'd walked into the river. She and Saint could've drowned. Now we all watched her, looking out for anything odd. There had been nothing odd, apart from her zombie-like, medicated state. That had become normal. But since we'd been in New York there'd been a torrent of odd.

Because the foolish, mixed-up girl had stopped her meds.

I was trying to support and protect her, but sometimes she made it fucking hard. And what did protecting her mean? Letting her be herself and not be tainted by medication, or making her take medication and have her spirit shoved down? This was getting too hard. How did I know what was right and wrong?

I couldn't deal with the pressure anymore.

Saint was in my mind. Little Saint. Who'd never asked to be caught up in this mess. I wanted him. I did. I had no doubt about that. But—all the weight was on me. Protecting Saint, helping Rach, and fighting Mr. Rees.

"I don't know what to do." I breathed the words into the dark room, then my forehead fell on to my arms, which were crossed over and resting on my knees. I felt like getting dressed and going for a run. But I didn't want Rach to wake up when I wasn't in the room, especially when it was still dark. She'd worry.

But I always thought easier when I ran and right now I wanted to run really fast and hard. I bumped my forehead against my arms a couple of times, longing for the thought that was going to be the answer to everything. There was no answer. That was the truth. Rach was sick, she always would be. She'd been dealing with it her whole life. That was why she'd ended up trying to jump off a bridge into the East River when I'd met her. Now I was on the journey with her and I just had to deal with it too.

"Man up." I lifted up my head.

But it was hard.

I'd likened being with her to a rollercoaster ride ever since I'd met her, and rollercoaster rides were fun. Her ups and downs, and the challenges she'd made me face, moving back home, having Saint, they'd made me feel alive, made my adrenalin rush and my heart beat harder. She'd changed me. Helped me become the person I wanted to be. The flat, slow, dull path of Rach on meds had made me miss her highs, but now I wished the highs didn't go so far up, and the dips wouldn't be so radical. I wanted to get on a gentler ride with her, that still had thrills, but thrills that didn't scare me. Thunder-Mountain-style maybe.

I was tired. She was exhausting. Trying to watch out for her, never knowing what mood I'd face from minute to minute.

Lord.

Saint was on this rollercoaster with us too. How was he going to survive it as he grew up?

A disloyal thought struck through my head—that maybe Saint was better off without us.

It wasn't true.

Images of Rach over Halloween assaulted the treacherous idea. She'd knocked his little hand on a door and fed him his first taste of chocolate, full of pride, and then he'd laughed. He loved her, he loved us, no matter that we were really too young to be parents.

Maybe that was just it. I was young, and struggling with stuff I shouldn't have to face at my age. Maybe I just needed to live a couple more years and I'd get stronger.

But I loved Saint. And I loved Rach. My heart ached with it. The emotion clasped tight in my chest and my belly. But loving her didn't tell me how to help her, or how to be with her when she was sick.

I'd been out of my depth ever since she'd walked into that river. She hadn't drowned. I had. I'd spent the last few months fighting it. Pushing the fear away. She'd scared me. But I hadn't been able to show her any of that fear because what I'd needed to do was look after her—and Saint, while his mommy was too sick.

But I hadn't just pushed away my fear for her and Saint, I'd trapped it behind a wall so I had the energy to fight Mr. Rees. I'd shut it away because I couldn't cope with it. Because I had to be able to cope. There wasn't another choice. She couldn't cope with hardly anything, so I had to.

But I couldn't keep shoving my feelings away forever—not when she'd be sick forever. I couldn't run away or hide from this forever. But I still wanted to run right now.

CHAPTER TEN

Rachel

When I woke up, Jason was dressed and lying on the bed beside me. He hadn't woken me. I looked at the clock. It was twelve. I sat up. My limbs were really heavy and tears gathered as pressure at the back of my eyes. It was a crappy day for me to go to a faceoff with Declan. I felt shitty. It was a low day. But I had to do it—and we needed to be there by one. Declan had his meeting at two.

"Why didn't you wake me?" I got out of bed.

"Because you were sleeping, so you obviously needed to sleep."

"I bet you wanted to go for a run, though."

"I did, but it doesn't matter. It's more important you feel okay."

His voice denied what he'd said. His run did matter.

"But you like running. It's important you get to run. You should've gone. You could've woken me."

He gave me a closed-lipped smile. He was off his game again today. But then his moods seemed to change with mine.

If you are… He'd said last night when I'd asked if he was happy.

He wasn't happy. The realization smacked at me.

"I'll get ready." I left him on the bed and went into the bathroom. I gripped the sink and breathed deeply, trying to breathe away the swamp of low energy that had settled on top of me. My head told me I wanted sex to escape it—to push this low feeling away, but Jason wasn't in the mood for me to jump him—and we needed to confront Declan. I wanted to keep Saint.

I washed, then dressed in dark jeans and a black sweater. Then I pulled my boots on as Jason sat up on the bed. He'd just been lying there watching me for the whole time I'd been getting dressed. When I slid my coat on, he got up and walked over to the closet, then put his sneakers on.

He was still silent.

He was really off today. I remembered thinking about his stiff posture last night. He wasn't happy, and he wasn't relaxed, and he was in an odd mood.

My head ran through a dozen images from last night; I couldn't think of anything I'd done wrong, or said wrong. But I was very good at doing things wrong. Maybe I didn't even know. Maybe he was wary of me getting things wrong today? He didn't want me to go.

When he put his arm around me as we stood in the elevator, his hand settled at my waist. It was reassuring—comforting. I leaned into him. I was a different person with him than I'd been with anyone else. I didn't want that to change. I wanted to keep him forever. I wanted us to be the fairytale, but today it didn't feel right.

His hand lifted on to my shoulder as we walked out of the elevator, then in the street he gripped my hand. I hung on to his, even when we walked through a busy crowd of people. I was hanging on to him because he was my sanity. He held me together, us together. Me, him, *and Saint*.

When we reached the office building, he looked back at me. "Ready for this?"

No. "Yeah." I'd never been to Declan's offices, he'd put me up in his penthouse for a year, but he'd kept me away from his businesses—and his wife.

The reception area was all cold and pale, shiny—clinical. Decorated in boring beige-stone tiles.

"Shall we walk up the stairs or take the elevator?"

"Stairs." It'd give me more time to get my head around what to say. I couldn't come up with any words, though, they'd slipped out of my head, and as we climbed the stairs the world shifted into slow-mo.

We stripped off our gloves at the top of the stairs and slipped them into our pockets, watching each other.

"Hey." Jason clasped my hand again, his cold skin against my cold skin. "I know you're down. We could go away and do this another day if you want? You don't have to face him today."

"No. I want to do it now." He was protecting me again. He knew I didn't find it easy to talk when I was down. But Declan knew that too. He'd know my threats would still count, even if I couldn't get the words out right. Declan, more than anyone, knew how vicious I could be and how hard I could fight when I wanted.

"Come on, then." Jason pushed the door open. He didn't look happy about going in there. But then he hadn't been at all happy for hours—days maybe—months maybe.

The office was open-plan and there were a couple of dozen people sitting at desks. I held on to Jason's hand harder, wondering where he'd sat when he'd worked here, as he led me across the room.

I saw Justin. He stood up and lifted a hand, but he didn't make any move to come over. Then I saw Portia as she swung her chair around to look at us. "Hi," she said as we walked past.

"Is he in?" Jason asked in a quiet, deep-pitched voice.

"Yes."

Jason looked ahead at an open door leading into the one office there was, at the far end of the room.

Declan had to be in that office.

I hadn't seen him since the night he'd shown up at Jason's apartment thinking he could trap me into going away with him, and before that, since the night I'd realized I'd hated what I'd become and decided to get away. The night that I'd stabbed him, to stop him forcing me into having sex. I hadn't wanted him to touch me anymore. I'd smashed a mirror and stabbed him with a shard of it, in a moment of madness, when I was trying to get away.

My heart pumped hard and my limbs were heavier as we walked toward the room.

I could see Declan. He didn't look up. Icy breath ran through my middle. The angel of fire had gone.

Jason didn't hesitate, he walked in and pulled me with him. Declan was sitting in a chair on the opposite side of a shiny, dark wooden desk.

I knew him intimately and he knew things about me Jason would never understand. He'd been attracted to my mood swings, he'd found my extremes and my recklessness when I was high fascinating. They were the only reason he'd been interested in me for longer than a week. He'd known he could persuade me to join in all the games he'd wanted me to play with him and his friends, and he played with my moods like I was a game.

He'd used me and abused my sickness.

He hadn't cared about me. But then I hadn't cared about him—I'd just been too sick to know right from wrong.

Jason's grip held tight around my hand, but he didn't try to speak. He left the speaking to me.

I pulled my hand free from Jason's, turned and pushed the door shut. I couldn't lean on him in here, and I needed a moment more to think.

When I turned back, Jason's hands slid into his pants pockets. He stared at Declan, but Declan stared at me.

"I'm going to have to get a security guard on the door of this office. Hello, Rachel. I didn't know you were in New York too."

His voice was light and mocking, and his tone implied that if he'd known I was here, he'd have come looking for me. I didn't want him to look for me. That was why we'd made sure our lawyer was in a city as big as Portland, and that he never included our address in any communications.

"How can I help you, Rachel?" Declan added, with a condescending pitch.

"You can stop fighting to take my son."

"Our son."

"My son, mine and Jason's." It felt so good to say that to Declan's face. Saint was mine and Jason's. I hadn't wanted Declan's kid. I didn't want anything more to do with Declan. I'd kept Saint because he was mine, part of me. Declan had never come into the decision or my mind. He only even knew about Saint because Jason had wanted to do things the right way.

"He hasn't anything to do with him legally." Declan waved a hand in Jason's direction. "He's got no claim over the kid."

Declan was a bully and a bad man.

I bit my lip. I wanted the right words. The words that would convince him. "You don't want Saint. I know. You just wanna win a fight. Any fight. It doesn't have to be this one."

"The judge won't listen to you, if that's your argument. *He just wants to win…*" he mocked.

Jason's fingers threaded through mine, holding on to me again. Telling me he was there, and he had my back.

I lifted my chin.

Adrenalin danced in my blood. "I wouldn't say that to the judge, I'd tell him about our past and the things you made me do. I'd tell him everything. You wouldn't just lose Saint if I did that. You'd lose your other kids, and your precious businesses and possessions."

He laughed.

The shithead

Violent anger roared into life in my head, like a match touched to gasoline, screaming at me—screaming at him. I hated him. My hand itched for that fragment of mirror to stab into him, over and over; to pay him back for all the times he'd assaulted me.

"Well, that's stupid," he mocked again. "How do you intend to win like that? You'd look worse than me. You'd lose the boy. He'd end up in the social system somewhere if you said all that. You're being foolish." Declan's eyes widened at the end of his words, and his eyebrows lifted, marking his point.

I'd forgotten how he used to treat me like stupid white trash. But he'd forgotten just how stupid I could be.

I stepped forward. "Do you think that would stop me? Saint wouldn't go into care; Saint would stay with Jason! And his parents! Saint has a safe home!"

There was a glass of water on Declan's desk. I picked it up.

Normal people would've thrown the water. I threw the glass and the water. It hit his chest, then dropped on to his leg as he pushed the chair back, it fell on to the floor when he got up. The glass didn't break but it must have hurt him, and his shirt and his trousers had gotten wet—he had a meeting in a half-hour.

I turned to go out, to get away from Declan. When I walked past Jason, I pushed his chest, knocking him out of the way.

I walked through the office, focusing on the door at the end, and when I was through it, I ran.

The door at the top of the stairs banged a second time. "Rach!"

I didn't stop running.

"Rach!"

I shoved the door open and ran into the reception area. I needed to get out of this fucking building.

"Rach!"

I pushed the next door open to get out into the street.

A hand grasped my arm. Jason's.

Tears blurred my view of his face when I turned.

"It's okay." His arms circled me and held tight. The panic eased, and the screaming in my head fell silent.

Everything was okay. He was here. Like he'd been the first night I'd run away from Declan. I wrapped my arms about his waist and ignored all the people on the sidewalk around us.

His hand stroked over my hair. "Why did you say that, Rach? You wouldn't want to leave Saint…"

People walked past us—him holding me didn't stop the world, or time—or Declan taking Saint.

I pulled away, breaking free from the sanctuary he'd given me for a whole year. But Jason knew me and he knew I'd do it just as much as Declan did—I'd risk it to keep Saint safe. "I would, if it stopped Declan getting him. Why did he have to do this?"

"Because he's a self-centered, jealous asshole. You know it and I know it." He'd used those words to make me laugh. I cried.

"It's okay." His arms wrapped around me once more.

But it wasn't okay. Losing Saint wasn't okay. "No." I broke out of Jason's arms. "We have to find Declan's dealer! We have to get Declan arrested!"

Jason's cell vibrated in his pocket. He took it out and looked at the screen. "Justin says, are you okay? Portia's just been told to go out and buy Mr. Rees some new clothes."

Oh my God. Jason hadn't succeeded in making me laugh. But that did. It was a weird, crazy laugh, but it came from my belly. It was the thought of Declan, in his office, in his business persona, soaked by the nightmare girl from his hidden life. He'd hate it, no matter that he'd taunted me.

Jason smiled, suddenly and broadly, in the way he'd have smiled at me last year, when we'd first met, when he was uncertain of me but learning to like me. When we were becoming friends. His smile collapsed just as quickly. Then he shook his head as he looked back down at his cell to text something back.

"What did you say?"

"That you're okay, but we have to find out who his dealer is and I've asked Justin if they want to meet us for dinner at Joe's tonight. We can put our heads together again. There must be something we haven't thought of yet."

"Sorry." The word slipped out as I looked at him.

A line formed a frown in his forehead and his lips twisted. "For what?"

"For putting you through this."

Scarlet red bloomed in the skin covering his cheekbones, and his brown eyes looked more fluid.

' Are you unhappy?" The thoughts I'd had yesterday spun around in my head.

He breathed in, like he was thinking of the answer. "No." But he'd had to think. Why had he had to think?

"Do you regret finding me last year?"

"No." That answer was fast and spoken with an assertiveness that denied it entirely.

"Thank you."

"You don't need to say thank you or sorry to me. We're in this together. That's all. Come on." His arm surrounded my shoulders. "Let's go to Central Park for a walk. We can go to the zoo or something, forget about *him* and take pictures to show Saint."

CHAPTER ELEVEN

Rachel

When we walked into the hotel lobby, Jason went over to the desk. We'd spent two hours walking around Central Park in the cold, all wrapped up in hats, scarves, and gloves. He'd been quiet, but then I'd been quiet too, as we took lots of pictures to share with Saint, so we could teach him what animal was what.

"Have you got any mail for me? It's Mr. Jason Macinlay."

The woman turned around to check, then turned back holding out a small packet. "Yes, sir, it arrived today."

"Thank you." He took it from her.

"You're welcome."

"What is it?" I turned with him, and we walked away.

"It's not for me. It's for you." He held out the packet.

I took off my gloves, shoved them in my pocket, and took it.

He pressed the elevator call button. The doors opened straight up.

"What is it?" I asked again as we walked into the elevator.

"It's from Mom."

I leaned back against the side and tore the edge of the packet open. My medicine. I looked up at him. A blush burned in my skin.

His eyebrows lifted. "Did you think I couldn't tell? When did you take them last?"

"Halloween."

"Why did you stop taking them?"

A need to defend myself swept in, a feeling I'd never had in response to anything Jason had said or done before. "Because I hate taking them. You said you missed the old me too. I hate feeling like a zombie. It isn't me. I don't like me on them."

He sighed and looked up at the lights in the ceiling. It was like he was disappointed, or despaired of me.

The walls I kept about me, to shut others out, to stop them hurting me, set up another, higher, layer. I didn't like him judging me. Jason was the one person who never judged me. Jason was the one person I didn't need to keep outside my walls.

He looked back at me. "Rach, I never suggested that you stop taking your meds. You know damn well I wouldn't have agreed if you'd told me. That's why, I guess, you didn't." He sighed again. "Look, I'm not going to make you take one, it's your choice. But remember why you were on them."

A part of me wanted him to make me take one. I knew I'd been going a little crazy. But I didn't want to make the choice to kill all the energy and emotion in me. Even if I made bad judgments.

The elevator doors opened on to our floor. I didn't know what to do or say. What did he want me to say?

He didn't say anything as we walked to our room.

He unlocked the door with the card key, pushed it open, and stood back to let me go in. He usually touched my ass or my waist when I walked through doors; this time he didn't. Now I knew why he'd gone quieter and less smiley on me yesterday. He was unhappy. He'd said he wasn't when I'd asked outside the office, but he was.

What did he expect me to do? What was he thinking?

When I got into the wide part of the room, where the bed was, I turned around. "Why aren't you shouting at me?" I wished he'd do that, but he hadn't even shouted when he'd found out I was pregnant with Saint, after we'd just started dating. Shouting, meanness, or aggressiveness, weren't Jason. That behavior wasn't in him. He couldn't do it. He couldn't be that person.

And I didn't know how to argue with him. How to make him tell me what was going on in his head…

"Should I be shouting? Should I be angry? Would it make any difference?"

Please shout! Then I'd know what to do. I'd shout back. But… If he did shout it wouldn't make anything different. "I don't know."

He walked past me and sat down on the bed, leaning forward and resting his elbows on his knees. He gripped his head for a moment then let his hands fall down to his thighs. "I don't think it would make anything better or worse."

"You aren't happy. You lied."

He looked at me. There was an odd expression in his eyes.

"Maybe, I don't know, Rach…"

"What?" I didn't know what to do. He'd never acted like this with me before. "You're confusing me."

"I don't know how to help you. I'm not a doctor. But I know when we had sex in that club the other night it felt wrong. You weren't thinking about me. That wasn't about us. You didn't have sex with me because you loved me. It was the same the other day, here, after I'd gone into the office the first time, wasn't it?"

I didn't answer. I didn't know how to answer. He'd been holding on to this. Thinking about it for two days—judging me…

"I don't like you when you're like that. I don't like it when you don't value yourself. You know I don't. I respect you. I want you to respect you too. I don't want to feel like I'm using you, Rach."

"I do value myself. I value who I am with you—"

"I… It doesn't matter." He stood up. "I'm going out for a run."

He was running from the argument. It was what Jason did. "Shall I come? Do you want me to come?" I didn't want him to run away from me.

"No, Rach. I'm sorry, I need some time on my own."

I need some time on my own… He'd never said that before.

He slipped his leather jacket off and threw it on to the open suitcase, then took off his top and threw that down too. He toed off his shoes, and then went to a drawer to pull out some clothes to run in. He took them into the bathroom to get changed.

I sat down on the bed, the open parcel with my meds in it still in my hand.

I heard him use the toilet and flush it, then change.

He came out a few moments later and searched for his earphones. I didn't speak to him, I had no words in my head. I was lost. He was unhappy with me.

He turned to look at me when he put his cell into his hoodie pocket. "I'll probably be about an hour." He put an earphone in one ear.

I nodded.

"Sorry, Rach."

I nodded.

"I just need some time to run and think things through."

I nodded.

He turned away and put the other earphone in, then walked out. He'd never walked away from me like this before, not when I was so upset. Not once.

I'd lost him. And he hadn't just walked away, he was running away.

Unhappy with me…

I'd lost him.

I sat down on the bed, tears clogging up in my eyelashes, as a sob escaped my throat. I spoke to his mom when I felt down. I couldn't call her. But I needed to talk to someone or I'd go completely insane. I stood up, put the parcel down, and dug my cell out of my purse. Lindy…

I looked up her number and called her. My hand shook as I held my cell against my ear.

"Hi, Rachel."

"Hey…" Now that I heard her voice I couldn't speak.

"Are you okay? How's it going?"

No, I wasn't okay. "Badly." Some people would think it very weird that I turned to my husband's ex for friendship, but they had not lived our lives. Lindy was the only true girlfriend I'd ever had—I could talk to her.

"Why?"

"You'll hate me and say I deserve this." Tears tracked down my cheeks.

"Why?"

"Jason's had enough of me. He's gone."

"He wouldn't walk out on you." There was shock in her voice, but the statement was adamant.

"He's mad at me. He's gone out running."

"Oh, he always goes running when he can't deal with something, we both know it." The relief in her voice said, oh, that's okay, it's not really a problem then. "Don't let it worry you. It's his thing, he did it every time we used to argue, and then we used to argue about that. It used to annoy the hell out of me."

"Who are you talking to?" I heard Billy, her boyfriend and Jason's best friend, shout in the background.

"Rachel! She's upset, things are going badly and Jason's gone out running and left her alone!"

"Tell her he'll be fine when he comes back! He probably needed some time to think things over!"

"Did you hear that?"

"Yeah."

"I told you at Halloween, he won't let go of you or let you down, he loves you." Lindy knew how vulnerable I was, because when I'd gone into the hospital we'd bared our souls to each other. Her mom had been sick and dying and Lindy had needed a girlfriend to confide in as much as I had, someone who understood what depression was like.

"He said he's not a doctor, he doesn't know how to cope with me."

"You know that's not true. What do you think?"

"That he's perfect for me. That I couldn't live without him. But he doesn't have mood swings and do stupid stuff. He can't understand me. Why should he stay with me?"

"Because he loves you, and he can't say he didn't walk into your relationship with his eyes open. It was pretty obvious you suffered with depression when he met you on the bridge."

Lindy was opinionated. She said things how they were. She was the opposite of Jason. It was no wonder they'd not made it. But us… "But that doesn't mean he'll keep on putting up with my moods. I'm hard work—" He'd judged me. He wasn't happy.

"And you're right Jason's the best person for you. He can deal with that. His patience is endless."

"Is Rach really upset?" I heard Billy. "Can I speak to her?"

"Do you mind?" Lindy asked me.

"No. Put him on." Billy probably knew Jason best, they'd been friends since they were kids.

"Hi. Why are you worrying?"

"He isn't happy, and I've never seen him like he was—"

"How was he?"

"Silent. Angry underneath. Frustrated with me."

"I've known him like that plenty of times. You'll be okay, he's a thinker, give him a chance to get his thoughts in order on a run and he'll come back in a better mood, and everything is gonna be fine. I promise. I'll hand you back to Lindy."

"He's right, Rachel. Honestly, I promise, it'll be okay. Just trust him."

"Okay." I didn't feel better. Fear hovered in the room, buzzing like a swarm of bees.

I do trust Jason! I yelled the words at myself. But paranoia was another part of my illness and it whipped at me like a wet towel, full of threats. "Thanks, goodbye." I ended the call abruptly. I couldn't talk anymore. The noise in my head was too loud.

A message made my cell vibrate. 'Are you okay, really? Call

again if you need to. You've got to keep talking if you're getting down x Lindy.'

She understood depression. 'I'll be okay.' I wouldn't go back to Manhattan Bridge. I had Saint at home. But a sudden desire to do it swept through me. I could even see the water, a long way below me, sparkling with the city's lights. Then I saw bright clear water, sparkling in the sunshine…

I looked up Jason's mom's number. "Hey, Mom." If I lost Jason, I'd lose his family too. They'd become my family. I hadn't had a mom and dad until his had accepted me. "May I speak to Saint?"

"Of course, sweetheart."

I rubbed the cuff of my sweater over my cheek and under my nose, wiping up the tears, and sniffed.

"Saint, speak to Mommy," Jason's mom said.

"Hey, darling." I breathed into the cell. "How are you?" Did Jason still want Saint?

Saint's breathing seeped through the cell, then there were babbling sounds, the elements of sounds that would become words. I'm sure he thought they were words. I wanted him to laugh. I wanted to hear his laugh so much.

"What are you doing, playing with Grampy and Granny? Did Grampy sing to you? No. I bet it was Granny who sang to you."

More babbling and breathy sounds.

"I'll be home soon. I promise, with Daddy. For good." That was all I wanted, to be with Jason and Saint—a family. So did it matter what mental state I was in?

Did it matter if I was doped up?

But I couldn't even feel happy on the meds. I felt miserable on meds. I wanted to feel happy sometimes.

"I love you," I said into my cell and blew a kiss.

"Could I speak to Jason?" His mom came back on.

"He isn't here. He went out for a run." My voice caught with an edge of tears as more leaked on to my cheeks. I wiped them up on the sleeve of my sweater.

"Oh." She sounded surprised, she knew it wasn't normal for him to leave me in a situation like this. "How are you?"

"Okay, thank you. Goodbye, Mom." I couldn't talk to her. I hadn't called to talk to her. I'd only wanted to hear Saint. I threw my cell on to the bed beside me and tumbled back, letting the tears flow, sobbing with self-centered pity, a massive dollop of paranoia, a scoop of insanity, and a one-ton weight of insecurity.

I hated bipolar and I hated Declan, but neither thing was going away, so how did I cope?

How would I cope alone, if Jason left me? I wouldn't.

CHAPTER TWELVE

Jason

I was breathing hard and sweating lots when I ran back toward the hotel, I'd gone a long way and I hadn't just been jogging. I'd been full-out sprinting most of the way, dodging through the New York crowds. I longed for the quiet open spaces of Oregon to run in. For Saint to pick up and squeeze. For life to go back to something that felt like normal. But there would never be a normal life with Rach. That was what I had to get my head around. And the abnormal was never going to be how I wanted it to be, her bipolar was unpredictable. It could go any direction for any reason, any moment.

Shit. Normal. Fuck. What did I think normal was?

Maybe that's what I'd been doing wrong. Fighting to reach something fixed and steady with Rach when it was impossible.

This up and down, and sometimes knocked out on meds, and sometimes crazy to the point she terrified me and made it painful to love her, and sometimes crazy to the point she made me love her more and made me crazy too, was normal with Rach. What we'd been living was normal. My head just had to get that and stop measuring my life, and me and Rach, by everyone else's normal.

This was normal for us.

But it didn't mean I had to keep letting her past invade our lives. That was one thing that I could fix. I didn't have to get used to that. I'd ignored everything that'd gone on before the moment I'd met her because I'd seen straight to the core of Rach the very first night, when she'd been covered in blood, terrified and shattered to bits. I'd never judged her by anything other than the person I'd seen, the girl who'd desperately needed someone to give her a chance and care about her. I didn't care that she'd done bad stuff and made stupid choices. The only thing I cared about from her past was a tiny bundle of lovable joy back with my parents.

The ground kept shifting with Rach, it always would. Life was going to be like living on a fault line. Ground trembles were going to be normal. I was getting it straight in my head now. Running always did that for me. I thought as I ran. I worked stuff through. I could live on a fault line.

But there was one earthquake I wasn't going to let happen. Mr. Rees had to give up fighting, because I knew Rach well enough to know she'd really tell everything to a judge and risk losing Saint, but what she was forgetting—there was no way I was going to let her do it and risk losing her.

When I stopped running outside the hotel I doubled over to catch my breath as the adrenalin pulsed through my blood and throbbed in my muscles. When I straightened up, I took my cell out of my pocket to switch off the music. I'd had a text.

'There's a support network for people who have a family member with bipolar, if you need it. Lindy looked it up. Here's the link.' It was from Billy.

'What??????' I texted back. What the fuck was he talking about? Where the hell had that come from?

'Rach called, she said you were pissed off with her.'

Fuck. I shoved the door of the hotel open, and walked through, steeling myself for another encounter.

Fault line. The words slipped through my head.

I could cope.

But what now?

I stood in the elevator car riding up to our floor still breathing hard, although now it was as much from unease as exercise. I pushed the card key in the lock to get into the room. The door clicked loose.

She flew at me when I walked in. Shouting and hitting me. "You bastard! You fucking bastard! You don't love Saint! You don't love me! You lied! You lied!" She threw her fists at me as hard as her words.

Shit. I'd only wanted an hour to myself, to get my head straightened out. But looking at the clock I'd probably been gone two hours and she'd freaked out.

"Stop it," I said it with a firm voice as I gripped her arms. This wasn't her, it was her bipolar. It was just another way it could swing.

"You left me!" She thrust the words in my face, in a growl of accusation.

"Rach, I went for a run. I wanted to run faster than I can with you."

"You ran away from me!"

Fuck, it was partly true. "Not like that. I just needed a break."

"Why?"

"Because, Rach..." *You're fucking hard work and I'm human, and I have feelings too!* God and only two weeks ago, on Halloween, I'd told her I didn't care that she was hard work.

"Do you hate me? I wish we hadn't come here. I wish we'd never told Declan that I was having a baby, we could have just put your name on Saint's birth certificate. We didn't need to involve him. This is your fault." Her arm pulled free of my hold and then she thumped me again, on the chest, with the side of her fist. "I fucking hate you! Why did you make me tell him?"

I grabbed her wrist. "I don't even fricking know myself anymore!" Maybe it was the first time I'd shouted at her. I'd shouted in front of her but never at her.

She recoiled as her eyebrows lifted and her green eyes opened wide.

102

"You don't want Saint…?"

Her pitch had dropped from an accusation to a question. She thought that's what I was saying.

"You don't want us…?"

"God, Rach, no. I love you. I love you both." I hauled her against my chest and hung on to her as she tried to pull free to hit me again, and I said into the air above her head, "This is your sick-brain talking, not you, this is why you need to take the medication."

Fault line. I was dealing with it.

Anger turned to tears and she clasped my hoodie either side of my waist in fists, while her forehead bumped in a rhythm against my shoulder and she sobbed. "You're scaring me."

"I didn't mean to. I just needed some time out."

"I don't want you to want time out!"

"But, Rach, I have to find a way to deal with stuff the same as you do. This morning you told me I should have gone running."

"This morning was different, and I meant you should have woken me and taken me running, you didn't even want me with you."

I didn't answer. I hadn't. I'd needed a break, and she was right, I'd run from her for a little while—or at least from all the problems loving Rach carried around with it.

She didn't say any more as she cried on my shoulder. I stroked her back.

Neither of us talked about the huge elephant standing in the room alongside us, and it was bigger than me walking out—*what do we do about Mr. Rees?*

She pulled away. I let her go. Then she wiped her eyes and her nose on her sleeve. "You need to shower. What time are we meeting your friends?"

"Seven."

She nodded and turned away from me. It felt like she was turning away entirely; turning her back on me.

I didn't say anything. It would cause more trouble. I went into the bathroom and stripped off in there. I let the shower run over my head, and then I cried so my tears merged with the water. Even if she came in she'd never know. Yes, I did love her and Saint, but I wasn't sure loving her was enough forever.

I'd told myself I could live on a fault line, but how the fuck did I know? I wasn't coping now. I wasn't coping.

We were both quiet when we dressed to go out.

When she went into the bathroom to put her make-up on I had a look at the packet of meds. None were missing.

Shit.

I wanted her to make the choice. I didn't want to police her.

My hands were in the pockets of my leather jacket when we walked along the hall to the elevators. Rach gripped my arm. I wasn't silent to be mean, I just had too much spinning in my head.

When we got down to Joe's, Justin and Portia were there already, sitting at the bar, waiting for us.

"Hey," I said weakly. I'm sure Rach and I had carried an atmosphere into the room. If Justin and Portia didn't feel it then Joe must've. He'd known us last year, when I'd come down here to eat just to have a few moments of her company, and to see her smile at me, rather than stay home alone. Those had been the days when I'd been pretending to myself that I could keep Rach in the friend zone. I'd been kidding myself on that score, she and I had had something going from the first moment she'd looked me in the eyes, her gaze suddenly telling me she'd realized she should be wondering who I was and if I was safe.

"It didn't go so well, I take it." Justin put a hand on my shoulder briefly, in a gesture saying, hi, and expressing empathy. Rach was clinging to my other arm.

"Nope."

"What now, then?" Portia asked.

"I don't know, shall we order food and eat while we talk." Rach hadn't said a thing. It was a sign her mood had taken a roller-coaster dip right down. I couldn't remember if I'd told Justin about her bipolar. But whatever, they'd have to understand, because that's the way things were.

"Can we have a table?" I asked one of the waitresses who came past the bar.

"Sure." She turned around, reached over, and picked up some menus, then turned back and held out a hand to show us to a table. My gaze followed the way she was pointing and clashed with Rach's, she'd been watching me watch the waitress, who was a woman neither of us had seen before. There was hurt, jealousy, accusation, and disappointment in Rach's eyes.

Fuck. How was I going to deal with a lifetime of this?

I took my hand out of my pocket, wrapped my arm around Rach's waist, and steered her to the table. Then I held her coat at her shoulders so she could take it off easier. I handed it to the waitress and pulled out a chair for Rachel before I took off my coat and sat down. I was walking on fucking broken glass around her.

We ordered and I talked to Portia and Justin about everything other than our problem with Mr. Rees, while Rach sat beside me silent, looking at her glass of soda. I was talking to them like nothing was wrong, but inside the concern I'd tried to run off earlier grew into a giant.

"So what are you going to do, then?" Justin prodded.

Who the fuck knew? But he wasn't talking about what I was thinking about. I didn't know what to do about Mr. Rees either, though. Apart from spending the next week following him around. "I don't know. The only chance we have is to get the police to catch him buying drugs. He refused to be blackmailed this morning, so threats won't work, it's going to have to be action. We know he's still taking cocaine, we just don't know where or when he's buying it."

Rach suddenly sat upright. "I didn't think before. He always had full packets on a Friday." She looked at me. Her eyes had the glossy disengaged look she always had when she was low. That image of her eyes haunted me. I'd seen it the night I'd met her on the bridge and the night I'd found her in the park when she'd run away after nearly drowning herself and Saint. She always looked through me, and never really saw me when she was like this. The emotions of both those nights swayed around in me.

The first night I'd met her, I'd been reluctant to take her home, but she'd had nowhere else to go and it was freezing and I'd been brought up by parents who'd taught me to play the good Samaritan whenever the call arose.

That decision had changed my life in an amazing way. I'd found love like I'd never imagined and become a father. But in the summer, I could have lost both things, and those emotions hung low in the pit of my belly, stirring nausea. I'd never really faced the fear and shock from that night. I hadn't had time to. Rach had needed my strength. There had never been the opportunity for me to admit how much it had scared me…

"Do you think he bought stuff for the weekend?" she said quietly. I could hear her remembering things she didn't want to remember.

I clasped her hand as it lay on the table. "Maybe." I looked back at Justin and Portia. "So maybe we know what day he buys it. It would be a good guess. He'd get some in for the weekend, surely. So, let's target Fridays for a start and see if we can work out where he gets it, if he's getting it on Fridays."

Portia looked at Rach. There were questions in Portia's eyes. Rach's head turned so she could stare out of the window. Portia could see something was wrong. Maybe she thought Rach was being rude? I'd text Justin after, to remind him, or tell him, that Rach had bipolar, so they understood. I'd never let anyone judge her badly, I wasn't going to start letting that happen now.

"I manage his diary, business and non-business appointments; I'll see if there's any clues in it. Maybe I could work it out."

106

I smiled at Portia. I'd definitely gotten her wrong before when I'd worked with her. I should stop judging others, just like I didn't want others judging Rach. I was just as bad at making rash and wrong decisions as other people. Portia was still willing to help, even though she probably thought Rach was bad-mannered tonight.

"I bet he doesn't ask you to book an appointment to meet his dealer, though." Justin made a joke out of it.

Portia made a face at him. "No. But there may be something he does every Friday, or someone he sees. I'll look."

"You're not kidding, are you?" Justin said.

"No." She shook her head and gave him a broad smile that said she loved playing detective.

She was a nice girl and they were good together.

I ought to apologize to her, except she'd never known all the bad words I'd thought about her, so admitting them would do more damage than good. "You really think you can find out?"

"I don't know. I won't promise. But it's worth a try, isn't it?"

"Sure, for us it is. Thanks. I appreciate you helping. You're cool, Portia."

We ordered more drinks and talked some more about other stuff, with Rach sitting silent, and then at ten o'clock we parted ways.

When we walked back to the hotel, I gripped Rach's hand, holding tight, holding on to her like she'd hung on to my arm on the way to the restaurant. We were still silent. She wasn't well enough for conversation.

When she went into the bathroom in the hotel, I looked at her packet of meds, wishing she'd take one and wondering if I should force her to.

Thank God I'd made her an appointment for next week. I'd have someone to talk to about this and maybe they'd force, or encourage, her to start taking her meds again.

Right now, though, I needed Justin and Portia to understand.

107

I took out my cell and typed a text to Justin. 'Hey, buddy, I can't remember if I said, but Rach has bipolar. That's why she was so quiet, it's just how she is sometimes, when she gets down. I hope you didn't take it badly, she didn't mean it that way. Thanks for a good night, I enjoyed your company. Call me if Portia finds anything.'

I had an answer in moments. 'No worries. It was good to hang out.'

CHAPTER THIRTEEN

Jason

On Thursday Rach didn't wake up. I had a shower and dressed, like I'd done the other day. She still didn't wake. She was way down low and totally out cold.

I looked at her meds: they were lying on the nightstand.

What the hell did I do?

Next week was too far away. I was going to go nuts before then. My head was going to explode. I needed someone to talk to. To download to. I was going to end up as messed up as she was.

Pressure rammed me down. There was Mr. Rees; and the need to look out for Rach, constantly—always trying to say and do the right things around her so I didn't upset her; and my business that I'd left on the back burner at home.

I wanted my son to pick up and cuddle…

One day I was going to pop.

I thought about sneaking through the services stairwell to get up on to the roof. I'd stand there and shout across the city, to let off the steam in me.

I took a breath and sighed it out. Rach lay on her side with her arm over her head, breathing quietly.

Tears gathered in my eyes and welled over. I wiped them away. I was trapped under deep, dark black clouds and it was sunny outside. My eyes didn't see the sunshine. My hands shook when

I walked over to the window and moved the voile curtain aside to look out. Yeah, it was sunny. The clouds were in me.

Fuck. Something had to change, and Rach wasn't going to change, so I needed to if I was keeping her, and I *was* keeping her, because as much as she was hard to live with I wouldn't be able to live without her either. She and Saint were the sun in my world. Maybe that was why the clouds were dark, because my sun was missing; Saint was at home and Rach was too ill to shine.

God, I needed help. I needed some sunshine. It was getting too dark. In the summer when Rach had been ill, I'd still had Saint to hold on to as a light to guide me, but without him…

I wiped more tears away.

I picked my cell up and looked at it. Debating with myself. I didn't talk stuff out with other people, I never had. I internalized and over-thought everything. Those were the charges Lindy used to throw at me in an argument; Rach had never moaned at me for it. She accepted me for who I was, as much as I accepted her. That was the real reason we'd hit it off at first, because we got each other, and we hadn't tried to change each other.

But I couldn't carry this around with me anymore, the pressure of holding this in was too heavy. I'd burst if I didn't let it out to someone, and I couldn't let it out to the one person I'd choose to talk to because Rachel had enough to deal with without worrying about me getting sick too.

I brought up Billy's text stream and touched the link he'd sent yesterday, it opened into the Depression and Bipolar Support Alliance. There was a number on the webpage. I called it, looking down at Rachel. I wanted to walk into the bathroom and talk in there, but if she was going to hear me it was better that she saw me in here, so she knew I saw her listening, and I wasn't trying to hide.

"Good day, DBSA, how can we help?" It was a woman at the other end.

I didn't know how they could help, though. "I… I…" I almost ended the call.

110

"Are you supporting someone?"

"Yeah." Shit, the tears welled up and the emotion gathered in a lump of pain at the back of my throat.

"And you're having difficulties…"

Fuck, I felt like Rach, when she couldn't form a sentence. "Yeah."

"In what way?"

I took another breath, glad the woman knew how to break this down into bites of information I could answer. "She's stopped taking her medication, and I don't want to force her, but she's been doing random stuff, and crying, and now she's just sleeping."

"Long periods of sleep is always a sign that people are suffering an occurrence of depression, and it's common for people with bipolar to avoid taking their medication. You're not alone. What's your name?"

"Jason."

"Well, Jason, often loved ones support an individual to continue taking their meds. Many people with bipolar will believe they are better off without medication, because it makes them feel lower and they like the highs—"

"I like her highs too, though, in a way, when she isn't heading toward mania. We have fun together when she's feeling good."

"Some people can live without medication but others need it, it's all about learning what triggers events and working out how to respond—"

"How do they do that?"

"With the support of her doctors and the hospital; you don't want to take it on alone. It's hard supporting someone alone. Is there anyone besides you?"

I leaned back against the wall and slid down it, so I sat on the floor against it, with my knees bent up as I held the cell to my ear. "Yeah, my parents, some friends, and other family. We live with my parents, but we're away from home…" I told her about our aborted plans to move out.

"Well, it sounds like she's lucky she has you and your family."

I didn't respond. Compliments weren't relevant today. I'd caused the depressive state she was in—in my view.

"We argued yesterday. I had my mom send Rachel's meds to us, and I gave them to her yesterday, but I told her it was her choice if she took one. She didn't. She still hasn't. We're going through a paternity case over her kid, and we're losing, and I feel like I'm to blame, and meanwhile I have to keep facing what she's done in the past when she treated herself badly, and let other people treat her badly—and it hurts. I hate seeing her ill. I hate seeing her not care about herself, and I hate thinking about how she's been hurt in the past. I went for a run. I just needed to get out of here and have some time to deal with stuff on my own. When I came back she was angry and beating on me. She accused me of hating her."

Shit, now I'd started, the words and the pain came flowing out while I stared at Rachel's face hoping her eyelids didn't lift. I didn't want her to overhear, I wanted to be able to tell someone how I felt. But I didn't want to hide in case she did overhear and I needed to manage the situation.

"Do you know anyone else with bipolar?"

"Nope."

"Well, it's normal for people when they're having an occurrence; to say things they don't mean, and it can be cutting and hurtful. They lose their judgment of situations when they're at extremes. At worst they won't even know what they're doing or saying—"

"I know. In the summer she walked into a river with our son and nearly drowned them both, and I don't think I'm over it." My breath hitched. Tears welled up and ran over.

That was at the heart of things. Nothing had been right since then, and I hadn't spoken to anyone about it.

"Did that scare you?"

"Yeah." My voice was low and gravelly. I wiped my hand under my nose.

112

"How did you feel? How do you feel about it now?"

"Shit." A broken sound of humor escaped my throat. "I don't want her to be hurt, or sick or down, but I can't protect her... Can I? What if she'd died? Not deliberately, I know she wouldn't do that now, but accidently... When she never even wanted to leave me... What if Saint had died? What if Saint had died and she'd lived? She'd never have coped with that. She can't even forgive herself for having risked it."

"She sounds like a good mom."

"She is. She's a great mom."

"Are you upset because you argued, or upset because of what happened before?"

"I don't even know."

"Don't let these situations get you down. Or let them hurt you. In minutes, hours, or after a day or so, she might be telling you something that's so upbeat it'll have you crying with laughter. To support someone, you have to learn to ignore their shit."

Another broken sound of humor rumbled in my throat. "Should you be saying that?"

"I support someone too. My girlfriend is terrible, she yells. I've learned not to yell back. I agree with her and walk away. I just tell her she's having an episode and she needs to calm down. When her mood settles then we take a look at her meds if we need to."

I nodded, even though the woman wasn't in the room to see. The weight on my shoulders had lifted a little and the pressure didn't feel like I was going to explode any moment anymore. I didn't feel alone with this woman at the other end of a call. "Have you ever thought, how do I keep coping with this forever? We're married, but I don't know if I can do the right things for her forever. It's exhausting. I'm tired. I've only known her a year, and if I'm not coping now..."

"We all have those days, Jason. That's normal too, for caregivers, for everyone, not just people caring for someone with bipolar. Everyone gets down sometime. And depression isn't exclusive to people with bipolar; they don't get to own the rights to it.

"I've thought at times I can't do this anymore. I think most of us who care for someone who has bipolar have. That's normal too. It's hard work. You get through those dark periods by hanging on to the memories of the good times; the memories of the things that make you love that person. Then you come out the other side and things feel better, and you don't even really know how sometimes. Then it's easier to love them again."

I breathed steadily for a minute, thinking and not speaking.

"Do you love your Rachel?"

"Yeah." The answer was instantaneous, there was no doubt in me. "My fear isn't that I don't or can't love her, just that I won't be able to keep coping and helping her. I don't even know what I think. That I'll crack up or something… That I'll go nuts. I feel breakable. I feel like I can't be happy anymore because I'm too worried about her… I… I feel down…" I laughed. Rach got down. Her downs were different than this. "Stupid, isn't it? My down comes in a hundredth behind hers…" It didn't count. It couldn't count, because she was far worse and I needed to be there—

"And you're trying to be super-strong?"

Yeah, that was what I'd been about to say to myself.

"We're all weak sometimes. There ain't nothing wrong with it. We're human. Sorry to tell you that, but you're as breakable as the next person. Not like your Rachel, but in your own way. So, hey, from what I can hear down the phone I'd say you need to stop pretending that you're okay, and get some help. You've been through a lot, and didn't you say there was some fight for her son too…?"

"Yeah, and it's dirty."

"Well, I'd suggest first of all you make sure she knows how much you love her, and that you'll be there for her. It sounds like you two have got a lot on your plate. But second of all tell her this; you need her to help you, you need her to take her medication to make things easier, and third, you talk to her about how you feel too. She needs to know. You can't hide it. She'll be sensing it. Bipolar doesn't make people stupid."

I smiled into the cell. I liked this woman.

"…Then when you get back home set up some support for yourself. We should have a support group that meets near you, so you can talk to other people who are supporting relatives. It's always easier if you can talk to someone who understands. And there are Facebook groups too, so there are other immediate routes if you're in the middle of a tough time."

"Thank you."

"Do you feel a little better?"

"Yeah." I did. "I guess."

"Do you want to keep talking? Is there anything else you wanna discuss or share?"

"Nope. I feel better knowing it isn't just me." A note of croaky, quiet, but almost proper laughter left my throat, because that was obvious; Rach was not the only person who had bipolar. "Thanks, you've helped."

"You can call anytime. That's what we're here for, to help people in your situation."

"Thanks."

"Don't forget to get in contact with a local group when you get back home and remember: to look after her you need to look after yourself."

"Yeah. Cheers."

"You're welcome. You take care of yourself now. Goodbye. Go give your Rachel a cuddle." She ended the call.

As soon as she'd gone the tears came back, running on to my cheeks. I sniffed and wiped them on the cuff of the hoodie I wore. But they wouldn't stop falling. I leaned my head back against the wall and let them come. Maybe fucking crying would release some more of the pressure.

I didn't know if I was crying for Rach or me, but it felt like the tears had been bottled up in me since the summer. I'd wanted to cry the night I'd found her in the park; I hadn't because I'd been holding her, and the next night I'd been holding Saint, and from that moment on, I'd always had one or the other to hold up so I'd never had time to let myself fall.

When the tears stopped I sat there breathing slowly. The weight on my shoulders had gone, and some of the tension in my chest had released. I still felt lonely, though, but stronger. Like I'd had my batteries recharged. The lack of pressure inside me was like someone had let some of the fizz out from a bottle of cola. That sound of air escaping, psssst, caught in my imagination. My tears had let the pressure lock go. I could cope. I would cope. If I found some help.

I got up off the floor, breathing in and out steadily because my heart beat with a crazy rhythm. Then I walked into the bathroom and washed my face. I didn't want Rach to know I'd had a meltdown. She was paranoid enough. But when I looked at myself in the mirror, I knew what that woman had said was true. I was breakable and I needed to admit that to someone and stop internalizing all my shit, and ask for help. I'd been trying to be Rach's superhero, but I didn't have any magic powers and I wasn't invincible. The woman was right; I was just human.

When I went back into the room, Rach was still asleep. She wouldn't get up today, I'd faced days like this with her at home when she was pregnant, and after Saint had been born. She'd been on lower medication and then none when she'd been breastfeeding. That was what had brought on her excursion into the river.

But if she wasn't going to wake up I needed to do what the woman had said and look out for me. If I stayed in the room with Rach I was going to go stir-crazy and climb the walls. I wanted to run.

No. I had to run.

I needed running to let go of all the shit piling up on top of me.

I got changed in the room, watching Rach as she slept, then went over to the narrow desk opposite the bathroom and scribbled on a piece of hotel paper, with the pen they'd left there. 'I've gone for a run, Rach, I need some air and exercise, that's all, don't worry, I'll be back soon xxx, I love you, Jason :-) .' I left the note on the nightstand and moved her cell over to there so she had it if she wanted to call me.

Then I put my earphones in, hung the Do Not Disturb sign on the outside of the door and left her, my heart thumping.

It was the first time I'd left her alone in that state. I didn't know if it was right or wrong to do it. But I needed to run. The woman was right. I'd be in a better condition to look after her if I looked after myself. I could cope if I had time to run. I ran fast, like I had the day before, challenging myself and pushing harder and harder. My breathing formed a hard, fast rhythm, like my feet hitting the asphalt as I ran along the sidewalk, then over Manhattan Bridge. I ran past the place where I'd found Rach.

That day she'd been so low she couldn't even remember how she'd gotten from Mr. Rees's to the bridge.

The woman was right. Rach had to be on meds, for her safety and for the safety of the people around her, and if she was too sick to make the choice, I had to. I was going to have to be the meds police. It was better that she was safe and dopey than dangerous and hurting, and I loved her whatever—it didn't matter if we weren't having a ton of exciting sex—God, when I'd been with Lindy, I'd hardly had sex, I hadn't even really discovered it until I'd met Rach. I could live with a slower sex life. I didn't like Rach dragging me into restrooms anyway, not when it was only done because she was sick.

As I kept running, I worked out in my head that the answer was simple. All I had to do was keep loving her.

When I got back to the room I was sweaty and hot, she wasn't awake, and she didn't look like she'd woken. I opened the curtains, to give the room a lighter atmosphere, took my earphones out and left them and my cell on the nightstand. She didn't wake.

I went into the bathroom to have a shower, then changed into jeans and a top. When I came back into the room I decided the time had come. I had the inner strength to wake her up and hold it together; she'd never guess I'd fallen to pieces.

I picked up her meds, poured a glass of water and put them beside the bed. Then picked up my cell and looked up the video I'd made of Saint laughing at the worm in a can we'd used as a Halloween trick. God, I loved his laugh. It filled my soul and gave me energy. I sat down on the bed beside Rach and played it near her ear. Her eyelids moved, as though she'd heard it.

I played it again.

Her eyelids lifted and her pale-green, mossy eyes looked at me. I stroked her blonde hair behind her ear. It was lank today because she hadn't gotten up and washed it. "Saint," she breathed.

She was really bad; her brain had gone into shutdown. She was talking through a dense oppressive fog, I could see it in her eyes. "He's not on the phone, it's the video. I wanted you to wake up. I want you to take your meds." I took a breath. "For me… Because I want you to be well, and you aren't well at the moment."

She didn't answer, just looked at me, but I knew she didn't have the energy to move. I touched the play icon again in the hope that the sound of Saint's laughter would seep into her brain and change her mood. I put my cell down, leaving it to play, and popped a pill out of the packet.

I lifted her head and shoulders, with an arm around her, and put the pill in her mouth. She obeyed my commands without a battle. I gave her the water and got her to take a sip to wash it down. She lay back down then and started crying and trembling.

I slipped off my shoes and walked around the bed, then lay down beside her, wrapped an arm around her and pulled her close, so her head rested on my chest. She continued crying and shaking.

Bipolar was a sickness, the same as MS or cystic fibrosis, or anything else more physical, and if she had something physical I wouldn't hesitate in committing to support her forever. I'd married her in sickness and in health. Just because this wasn't something physical but mental, and I couldn't see it, or manage it easily for her, I'd been letting it scare me. I had to stop letting it scare me. So, yeah, I'd go to a group and admit I needed help.

I'd faced everything in life head on, I tackled stuff, chucked myself at it, ran at it. I'd been brought up with a belief that hard work always won out. But if I needed to work hard and be strong for Rach and Saint for the rest of my life, this wasn't something I could run at. If I put all my energy into it, I was going to burn out. I needed to recharge. I had to support me too. I'd been working hard to fix things, but Rach's illness wasn't fixable. The solution was accepting how it was. I'd never make Rach better, but I could love her, happy or down, and while I did that, I had to be me, strong or weak, hurting or happy. None of those emotions were wrong; they were just going to be a part of the fault line I'd chosen to live on.

I felt better with a plan.

She fell asleep on my chest. I lay quiet and held her.

People with a physical condition could pop a painkiller and it would take away the pain within an hour; Rach's pills would take days to work again. Bipolar was not a nice thing.

She woke up at five o'clock and suddenly leaned up on one elbow, her palm settling on my chest. "Have I slept all day?"

"Yeah."

"Sorry."

My fingers stroked through her hair. "You don't have to be sorry for being who you are."

"You'll make me cry."

"It's okay if you want to cry, if crying makes you feel better."

She sniffed and did start crying. I laughed. Which perhaps was

119

a bit inappropriate, but it was funny the way her tears had switched on when I'd given them permission.

"You're laughing?"

"Yeah, I feel better. Do you remember I gave you your pill?"

She shook her head.

"Well, I did, and I'm going to keep giving them to you, and watching you take them, so I know you've had them, because I want you to be okay. I love you and I don't want to see you going through what you've been going through since we've been in New York."

Her forehead dropped against my shoulder and she hugged me. "I love you too."

I smiled, then started moving. "Come on, get up. You can argue with me about your meds when you feel better, if you want. I know you're not up to anything now, but, for the record, you won't win anyway so you may not want to bother trying. I'll run you a bath, you can have a soak that'll make you feel a little better, and I'll call down for room service so we don't have to go out, then we can chill out up here and pick a film."

She nodded as I climbed off the bed.

I went into the bathroom and started running the water for her.

"Hey, Mom. Can I speak to Saint?" The words were said quietly.

I walked back into the room. She was lying down with her cell to her ear.

"Hi, darling, it's Mommy," she whispered into the cell. "I love you."

She was silent, for a moment, then—

"Hush, little baby, don't say a word, Papa's gonna buy you a mocking bird." Her voice was really low and husky from sleep. It was beautiful and entrancing—like her. "And if that mocking bird won't sing, Papa's gonna buy you a diamond ring, and if that diamond ring don't shine…"

She was terrified she was a bad mom. She wasn't. She was a wonderful mom. She loved Saint so much.

My heart swelled with the love I felt for them both.

I bent and clasped her foot through the comforter, and gave it a squeeze.

She gave me a little smile when she'd finished the song, then she was silent for a moment, and just listened, I presumed, to Saint's reaction.

She held the cell out to me. "Do you wanna speak?"

"Yeah."

I took the cell, and held it to my ear. I could hear him breathing. "Hey, trouble, it's Daddy. How have you been doing? Have you been keeping Granny and Grampy up at night?"

There was a slightly different sound, like Saint had listened and answered, in his baby form of talking, just different sorts of breaths. "I love you, buddy, I'm missing you like crazy. So's Mommy."

Rach watched me. I smiled at her, broadly, telling her, *I love you*. I'd recharged. I had the energy to deal with this. I did.

Mom came on the call. "Hello, darling. How are you? Rachel said you weren't there yesterday, she didn't sound well."

"She's doing alright. She's a tough girl. She'll be fine and we'll be home soon anyway, as soon as this is fixed." I'd refused to think all day about the fact that it wasn't fixed and there was no sign of it being fixed. I was going to fix Mr. Rees. I was going to run as fast as I could at it and fix Mr. Rees. That did not have to be like it was.

"I'm glad things sound okay, sweetheart, look after yourself and Rachel. Give our love to her."

"I will do. I love you, Mom. Thanks for everything you're doing." It was odd that she'd chosen those words, *look after yourself and Rachel*, but knowing me, she'd probably said that a hundred times and I hadn't heard what she'd meant.

"We love you too."

"Bye." I ended the call and put Rach's cell back on the nightstand.

She was lying there watching me.

"I'll check the water for your bath. What do you want to eat?"

"Do you reckon they'll have a grilled cheese sandwich?"

"If they don't have one I'll tell them to fucking go buy the stuff and make one."

She gave me a weak smile before I turned away to go and check on her bath. The water was deep enough, and warm. I tipped some of the hotel's shower gel into it and swished it around so it gave her some bubbles.

"Thanks." She was at the door.

I straightened up. "You're welcome."

"I'm sorry I shouted at you yesterday."

"That's okay, I know you didn't mean it."

"Are you still angry with me?"

"I wasn't angry with you then. I was struggling for a while. I'm okay now."

"Sorry." She came toward me. She only had her panties and a loose tee on, another one of my old ones that she'd adopted and kept since we'd gotten together. Her arms wrapped around my middle and she pressed against me.

My hand stroked over her hair. "I love you."

"Thank you—for loving me. I know I never ask how you are, but I do care… I love you so much…"

"I know."

I wrapped her up tight in my arms, hugging her right back, and gave her a squeeze like I did with Saint when I hugged him. *"I'd suggest that you just make sure she knows how much you love her, and that you'll be there for her… Go give your Rachel a cuddle."*

My cell rang in the other room. I let her go. "You get in the bath."

My cell was vibrating and ringing on the nightstand by the bed. I picked it up. The screen said Justin. "Hey. What's up?"

"Hi, Jason, it's Portia. I know something. I think I worked out where and exactly when Mr. Rees is buying drugs."

122

Oh Lord. "Yeah…"

"Yeah, he goes to a gym every Friday morning at eleven-thirty. He had it down as a business meeting, but I checked the address because it's the only constant he has on that day, and it's a gym and we know he's got a gym in his penthouse, so I'm guessing he isn't there to exercise."

My heart did a frickin' leap in my chest. "How good a bet do you reckon this is?"

"A very good bet, eighty percent…"

Shit. Had we caught him? "Thanks, Portia. What should I do? Is it safe to call the cops? What if we're wrong?"

"If it was me I'd call them anonymously, from a phone that can't be traced to you. Then if I'm wrong, there'll be no comeback. But I think I'm right. Can you imagine him stopping in a parking lot to pick up his fix? No, he'd go somewhere indoors, and somewhere he can be private without being obvious. What better place than a gym locker room?"

"Okay, I'll call the cops. Thanks again. You didn't have to help."

"You're welcome. You'll keep in touch this time, won't you? Justin missed you."

"Hey!" He shouted in the background.

"He did. He likes you. He doesn't have a guy to talk to at work since you left."

I smiled into my cell. "Tell him I'll keep in touch. I promise. But he does pretty good at talking to the girls."

She laughed.

She was okay. "What's the name of the gym? Where is it?"

I walked over to the desk and wrote it down on a sheet of hotel paper. "Thanks, Portia. I'm hoping you're going to see us next week, with any luck I'll be bringing the adoption papers in for him to sign."

"I hope so. I want this to come out good for you two, you deserve it."

"Thanks. You're a darling. Bye."

"Bye, Jason. Good luck." She ended the call.

I held my cell in my hand for a moment, staring at it, my fingers tightening and gripping it hard. Euphoria played with hope.

We had him!

Then anxiety kicked in. *Maybe* we had him. Anxiety danced around with uncertainty on the cloud of hope, and the air solidified in my lungs… This wasn't over yet. We needed the police to catch him.

"Jason! Who was it?"

I threw my cell on the bed "Portia!" and walked back into the bathroom. "She thinks she's got Mr. Rees pinned down."

Rach sat up, the water swaying around her. "Declan… How?"

"He goes to a gym every Friday at eleven-thirty, like clockwork."

"Oh my God." Her arms wrapped around her bent-up legs, gripping her knees. "What will you do?"

"Go down to the lobby and ask to make a call on their phone and give the cops a tip-off that someone is dealing drugs at this gym and I know there's an exchange going on with Declan Rees, who'll go in there at eleven-thirty." I smiled at her. "I'm going to go order your supper now, though. The cops can wait."

I left her and went back into the room. After I'd rung room service I went back in the bathroom and lowered the toilet lid to sit down and talk to her. "How are you feeling?"

"Whacked out, like I'm a corpse."

I smiled slightly, she was trying to be light-hearted. "I went for a run while you slept. I left a note by the bed in case you woke up."

She nodded. "I know you need to run. I'm sorry I told you not to."

I leaned forward and rested my elbows on my knees. She was still sitting upright with her arms wrapped around her legs. She'd sat in the bath like that the first night I'd met her.

"I called a support group too."

Her green eyes widened a little. I loved that unusual color.

"I spoke to this woman who told me loads of people with bipolar stop taking their meds. You aren't alone in hating them."

"You hate them too."

I sighed and cringed inside. She was thinking about our *I miss you* conversation over Halloween. I'd probably handled that all wrong. But I'd only been with her a year, I was still learning how to speak to her bipolar, I wasn't going to get everything right straight off. "I did. I do. Yeah. I hate that they hold you down. But most of all I want you to be well, Rach, and you aren't well when you're off the meds. The woman said you might get off them again later, people do, but for now, I should make sure you take them, so I'm going to."

"What else did she say?" Rach's tone was flat, maybe because she was low, or maybe because she was worried about me speaking to someone else about her—about us.

"That I should show you how much I love you and not listen when you rant at me."

Her lips twisted. It wasn't in a smile, but there was a hint of one.

"And that I should look after myself too, because if I'm going to help you, I need to help myself as much."

"I want you to be happy. I want you to love me. But I don't feel like you are or you do anymore." She said it quietly, as though she was afraid of saying it, in case it was true, and her eyes looked at me, windows into a soul that was in a lot of pain today.

I'd always love her.

"I told you on Halloween I did. I do. Please will you take it as given? I still love you, I always will, you don't need to worry about it. But sometimes I'm going to get tired and I'm going to find it hard. It doesn't mean I don't love you. Or that I want to give up. Just that for a short while I need space to deal with my own feelings, because sometimes I'm going to get down or angry, and, I admit, I'm not happy at the moment, but it's not because of you. Don't you dare let your brain start taking the blame for it. It's everything. It's gotten to be too much, that's all. They have a support group somewhere in our area; it's made up of other people who support someone with bipolar. I'm going to go when we get back home. I think it'll help me, so I can help you."

"Thank you."

"For what?"

"For putting up with me…"

"I don't put up with you, honey. I'm here because I love you."

She nodded, then her chin rested on her knees. My words hadn't sunk into her heart or her head. She was too ill today.

"Lie back and soak, I'll make you a coffee."

"Thank you."

The water stirred as she moved and I walked out the door. I felt calm.

When I was making coffee, there was a knock on the door; it was room service with our supper. I took our grilled-cheese sandwiches and coffee into the bathroom, then she lay in the bath eating and drinking as I sat on the closed toilet and ate. She was quiet, but not as bad as last night.

When I'd finished eating I got up and took my plate out to put it down on the desk in the room. The water stirred as she climbed out of the bath. I turned back to look at her. She wrapped a towel around her body.

"I'm going to go down to the lobby to make that call to the cops."

She nodded.

"I won't be long."

I took a clean hoodie out of a drawer before I left.

Instead of heading to the elevators, I went to the stairs and, out of sight of any CCTV cameras, I changed my top, flicked the hood up, and stuffed my other top down in a corner. If this went to shit I didn't want the cops tracing the call and tracking me down so they could charge me as a hoaxer.

126

I went down to the reception desk and tried to look like I was on my way out for a run or a walk or something. "Can I make a local call?" I pointed at the phone on the end of their desk.

"Sure thing, you're welcome to, but there's a phone in the office at the back you can use. That'll be more private."

"Thanks, I'll only be a minute."

The guy led me to the place where they managed the safety deposit boxes. There wouldn't be any CCTV in there either; they could hardly film people taking the stuff in and out of their boxes. There was a phone on the guests' waiting desk. "Here, sir."

"Thank you."

"You're welcome." He left me in there. I pressed 911.

"Hello, 911 Emergency Services. What's your emergency?"

"Can I speak to the police, please? I have some information they'll want to know…"

CHAPTER FOURTEEN

Jason

When we went to bed, Rach laid up close against me, with her head on my pec and her hand resting over my abs as I held her and watched movie after movie from the hotel box office on the TV. She'd drifted in and out of sleep in a half-comatose state. The last time I looked at the clock before I fell asleep it was ten past two.

I stayed in bed with her Friday morning too. In the same position, with the TV on more movies.

I'd spent a lot of hours in this position when she'd first come out of the hospital, only at home I'd had Saint laying across my chest too. I missed him; there was an ache of longing deep in my chest.

The digital clock on the nightstand flicked through the numbers as the morning progressed.

When the time reached eleven, my heart was beating so hard it was like I was running. Mr. Rees must be on his way to the gym.

I couldn't lie still anymore. I bent and kissed the crown of Rachel's head. "Do you want a coffee, and then you can take your meds?"

"Okay."

My hands fucking shook when I made her coffee while the clock's digits counted towards eleven-thirty.

I wished I'd gone to the gym and stood outside to see what happened. But it was better Rach and I stayed out of it and left it as a police matter; if we got caught up in it, it could affect the case. I didn't want to mess this up.

"Here." I put her coffee and her pill down on the nightstand beside her.

She didn't move, but the coffee was too hot to drink anyway.

I walked over and opened the curtain to look out. The street below was busy. I glanced back at the clock. Eleven-twenty.

Dammit, I couldn't stand still. I had to do something, my brain was too full of what might happen.

I picked up my cell from beside the bed and went over to turn the TV down.

Rachel watched me without talking.

Tomorrow would be Saturday, our lawyer wouldn't be in his office. I touched contacts and slid them up 'til I reached our lawyer's number, then touched the call icon.

"Hello, Goldman Law, how can I help you?"

"Hey, can I speak to Mike, please, it's Jason Macinlay?" I looked back out the window while I waited for her to transfer me.

"Hi, Jason. How can I help?"

"We're in New York. We came to see him. I'm going to get him to sign those adoption papers. Would you fax them through to the hotel?" I had to prepare as if this was going to go down as we'd planned. I had to have faith or I'd go mad.

"Sure, I can get them faxed through, but don't do anything stupid."

"I'm not going to. I'm relying on him doing the stupid stuff."

"Okay, where do I send the paperwork to?"

The hotel's fax number was printed on their notepaper; I went over to the desk and read it out, then gave him our room number. After he ended the call, I rang the reception desk to

129

tell them a fax would be coming in for us. Then I looked at the clock.

Eleven thirty-nine.

Would they arrest him when he got to the gym and miss any exchange? Would they follow him and watch him until it happened? What if it happened in a restroom cubicle and they missed it? What if they hadn't even responded to the warning and he was just now starting on a machine at the gym and nothing would happen?

I dropped my cell on the desk in sudden disgust. My hands lifted and gripped the back of my neck.

Fuck. I wished I knew what was happening. I looked up at the ceiling. But then I remembered Rach was awake, just quiet.

My hands dropped and I turned around.

She was watching me. Her pill was still beside the bed.

I went over to the bed. "Sit up, honey."

She leaned up on to her elbows first, then straightened up further, sliding up the bed until she was sitting up against the headboard. I sat beside her and handed her the coffee. "Here, sip it, then take your meds."

"Thanks." She wasn't saying thanks for the coffee. She was saying thanks for the care.

I gave her the pill and smiled at her. She took it, then sipped the coffee.

"We'll stay in the room today, okay?"

She nodded.

I looked at the clock as she sipped her coffee again. Eleven forty-five.

How were we even going to know if he was caught?

"Would you turn the sound on the TV up?" Rach asked.

"Sure." I got up and fetched the remote to do it, then went back over to her. "Do you want to sit up for a bit?"

She nodded.

130

It was going to be a long day.

I helped her put a couple of cushions and pillows behind her, so she could sit up comfortably, then I sat beside her.

It was twelve o'clock. I stood up and looked out the window again.

"Jason, go for a run if you want, I'll be okay here."

"Are you sure?"

"Yeah."

I didn't want to leave her, but running would make me feel better. "I wish you'd come with me but I know that's a dumb hope, because you aren't up to it today. I'd rather have you with me, though. Just for the record, Rach."

She shook her head, in a don't-be-stupid way. "You can go and don't feel guilty. I won't be nasty about it. I promise. I don't mind."

I put a knee on the bed, leaned over, and kissed her on the lips. "Thanks. I love you, sweetheart."

She gave me a weak smile.

I wanted Mr. Rees out of our lives, so she and I could carry on just having to think about us—and Saint.

I got changed, looking at my cell all the time. It didn't ring, or vibrate. I picked it up once. It still had a signal.

By the time I left the room, it was twelve-twenty. The appointment on his calendar had been for an hour.

Had they caught him?

I didn't run so fast today, I ran at a pace more like a jog, but I had a good rhythm going. I tried to let the movement, the adrenalin, and the world around me absorb my thoughts, but I didn't succeed. All I could think about was Rach lying quiet and exhausted, in a black mood, back in the hotel, and whether or not the police had caught Mr. Rees in the act.

My heartbeat followed the pattern of my footfalls on the sidewalk.

Come on. Come on. The words ran through my head. I

pictured the cops arresting Mr. Rees. It was my only hope of stopping him.

The digital clock in the room read one-forty when I went back in and pulled my top off, my heart pumping in a crazy beat.

Rachel was lying down on the bed again, asleep.

I showered, then lay own beside her. It was like someone had pressed a pause button; nothing could carry on until I knew. Was he in jail? Was he being questioned? Was he walking free, driving around Manhattan in his fancy chauffeur-driven car? How could I know?

I wanted to ring every fucking police station in New York to find out. But that would raise suspicions against me, and then maybe he'd claim he'd been set up. I didn't want to risk this going wrong… But had it gone right?

I got up to make a cup of coffee. To have something to do.

Rach woke up. "Hey." Her fingers reached out and brushed my hip, before I could walk away to make it. "Did you have a good run?"

"Yeah, thanks." I lay back down, on my side, so I faced her. My fingers combed into her hair.

"Have you heard anything?"

"Nope."

"Sorry."

I laughed a little. "I hardly think you can take responsibility for that."

She smiled slightly. "Can we have sex?" She said it quietly. "Not because I… Just… I love you, I want to do it with you. I want to feel loved again and I want to show you that I love you…"

My fingers stroked through her hair. "I love you too and I don't really mind if you have sex with me for whatever reason you want."

Another weak smile lifted the edges of her lips.

132

I got up and stripped off, then got into bed with her. We kissed slowly and I slid my hand beneath the tee she had on to grip her breast. After a couple of minutes, I stripped the tee off of her.

She was beautiful. Her body was amazing, all muscle and soft skin, and her long arms and legs wrapped around me.

We carried on kissing while I caressed her breast, squeezing it gently, and then my hand travelled down to slip inside her panties. Her hips lifted in a gesture of yes-please as her hand settled on the back of my head.

After I'd helped her out of her panties I moved over her. Her hands shifted down to my hips and held me there. "I love you," I said when I pushed into her. "I always will. You can trust me."

She gave me a weak little smile. "I know."

I looked down to watch myself slide into her as her legs lifted. Her inner thighs brushed against the outside of mine.

I made love to her slowly, looking into her green eyes, making sure she could feel the sensations and know that this was because I cared about her—she was my everything. She had shown me a life I hadn't known was in reach for me until I'd met her.

We lay in bed after, naked, with my arm around her, but she wasn't quiet, she talked to me, about Saint, about the future she hoped for, for him and for us.

My cell started ringing and vibrating, rattling on the nightstand beside the bed. I reached over and grabbed it, with Rach still tucked under my other arm. The clock said four-fifteen and the name on the screen said Justin. My heart drummed out a heavier bass beat than it had when I'd been running. "It's Justin," I said to Rach.

I touched the answer icon. "Hey."

"Jason…" It wasn't Justin it was Portia, and she'd whispered my name.

I sat up, my arm slipping free from Rach. "What is it?"

"Mr. Rees is in jail. I just got a call from his lawyer, to cancel a dinner he'd planned for tonight. He can't bail him out yet, he thinks it'll be twenty-four hours at least. He wouldn't tell me why, but I'm guessing they caught him buying cocaine." I could hear her smile through the cell.

"Yeah!" I roared as my free hand punched the air.

Portia laughed when I shouted.

"Thanks for letting us know, Portia. And thanks for helping. You're an angel. And you and Justin are going to have to fly to Oregon and come meet Saint."

"That would be fun. I have to go now, though, I'm still in the office. I'm calling from the restroom."

"I'll be in there on Monday. I'm going to bring the adoption papers in. I'm not going to give him any chance to think about this."

"Cool, get him before he can work out a way to get out of it, you know how slippery he is. Bye, Jason."

"Say hey to Justin."

"Yeah."

She ended the call. I turned to Rach, my cell clasped in my fist. "He's in jail. He's been arrested for something. Portia doesn't know why, but it has to be drugs. We got him."

Rach sat up and wrapped her arms around my neck. "Wow."

I hugged her hard. "Everything's going to be okay. See I told you."

"Thank you."

"You're welcome."

Even I actually fucking believed it.

That felt good.

My heart leapt with anticipation and anxiety when I looked at the text that had come in from Justin. 'He's in.'

He'd texted at nine to say Mr. Rees wasn't there, telling me not to bother taking the adoption papers over to the office. Now I could. "He's in, Rach!" I called into the bathroom.

All the paperwork was in an envelope on the desk.

I walked over to the bathroom, where she was putting on her make-up. "Are you sure you're up to coming? You don't need to." I wanted to get there. I wanted to fly there and get this over and done with. I wanted to be walking away with the signed papers in my hand, certain that everything was going to be okay. I didn't want to miss him…

She looked at me, her mascara brush hovering near her eye. "I want to."

"But will it throw you down again? If it will, I'd rather you stayed away."

"I can't know, but I wanna be with you."

"If you're sure."

She looked back at the mirror and applied her mascara, refusing to answer anymore.

I guess she was coming. After the other day, I wasn't happy about it, but I couldn't deny her, Saint was her son, she had a right to be there.

She'd recovered enough to run with me this morning, and that had pulled her further out of the blues, but she was vulnerable. She'd always be vulnerable, though, and I guess that wasn't a reason to stop her from living life as she wanted.

I put my leather jacket on, then picked up her scarf and coat. I wrapped her scarf around her neck when she came out of the bathroom, then held up her coat for her to put on.

My heart played out a low, steady rhythm.

"Come on." My hand settled on her waist as we turned to the door.

I was twenty times more protective toward her today. There were the same feelings inside me that had been there after she'd walked into the river. I wanted to wrap her up and push the world away from her. When I saw her in her weakest moments

135

it drove a wedge of compassion deep inside me, like it had the first night I'd met her, only then I hadn't loved her; now I loved her the wedge opened up a chasm of pain too.

My hand touched her waist, hovered near her, or held hers all the way to the office. I wasn't worrying over what Mr. Rees would do or not do anymore, not this time, I just cared about how this was going to impact on Rach.

Fuck him.

CHAPTER FIFTEEN

Rachel

Jason's body was barely an inch away from mine when we stood in the car on the subway, and he stayed close to me all the way to Declan's office, on hyper-drive protection.

When I saw the tall building that had once been where Jason worked, and was still where Declan worked, Jason's hand held mine. The grip was gentle—reassuring—offering a sanctuary—and love—a wall to defend me rather than a sword to help me fight. His grip said he treasured the thing he clasped.

Today there wasn't even a single grain of sand of doubt in me. I knew he loved me. But I knew my lack of trust would return with my next bout of madness. I wanted to hang on to this feeling, though. I wanted to be able to remember it when I was low.

I would let him keep checking that I'd taken my meds if it meant I felt like this. I'd returned from hell. But it would only be for a while if I didn't stay on meds. Hell was behind me, stalking me and waiting to take me down.

But I was free again today. The sky was blue and bright, and I had Jason's hand to hold, and I wasn't high, but neither was I really low. I was in limbo land, but today it was lovely.

Jason led me through the crowd. Like he'd led me through my madness—fixing us again.

We walked into the ground floor of the office block and rode the elevator up to Declan's offices.

In the elevator Jason let go of my hand. We stripped off our gloves, then his arms surrounded me. I pressed my face into his neck and breathed in the smell of his aftershave.

He let me go when the doors opened and then clasped my hand again and led me out. "Ready for this?" he said, looking back at me.

Nope. Not at all. But… "Yeah." I was gonna get Saint officially and forever. I was. He'd be Jason's son. Declan would have no claim on him, and Declan and the past that hovered around him would be out of my life.

"I love you," I said to Jason, in the form of a thank you.

He opened the door into the office, then smiled back at me. "I love you too."

We walked on, through all the desks and working people. I looked across the room to where Justin's and Portia's desks were. Justin stood up and lifted a hand, but then he turned away and walked over to a printer. I guess he didn't want to make a big deal of us coming back in; the people in the room must know I'd thrown water at their boss, a few of them stared.

Jason's hand gave mine a little squeeze as we neared Portia.

When we reached her he leaned down. "Would you come in with us? We'll need a witness to sign the papers and you're his PA, so it's a good call for you to do it, he can't blame you for getting involved."

"Okay." She stood up when Jason straightened.

The papers were inside Jason's zipped-up jacket, against his chest, near his heart. He loved Saint. I knew he did. We were in New York because he loved me and Saint. With a clear head I knew it in every cell of my body.

The three of us then, me, Jason, and Portia, a little posse, walked toward Declan's office door.

This was judgment day for him. The moment of retribution. He'd done me wrong and Jason was putting it right.

On Halloween I'd known we were falling apart and the only

way we could be put back together was if Jason chose to fix us. He had. He was picking up all my broken pieces and putting them back together again—so he and I could be *us* again.

Declan stood up when we walked into the office with Portia behind us. He glared at me but he didn't look so confident.

If he hadn't already known we were the ones who'd snitched on him, he knew it now.

Jason let go of my hand, undid his jacket zipper halfway, and pulled out the envelope containing the papers. "Any judge," he said, "who sees the psychiatric reports for Rachel will know that with the support of others, who'll make sure she takes her medication, she's going to be a great mom. But that same judge is going to look at reports on you being arrested for buying cocaine," Jason pulled the papers out of the envelope, "and he'll know that you're unfit to be a father. So just give up and sign these, and then we'll happily stay out of your life." Jason put the papers down flat on Declan's desk. "Your PA is here to witness you sign it."

Declan looked at Portia. He didn't like her being in the room. He looked at Jason. Declan had stuff he wanted to say, accusations maybe—rants, threats—but he didn't say them because Portia was there.

"You can have him. I never wanted the brat." He sat down, pulled the paperwork over, and flicked to the end of it. My heart pulsed into a rapid flaring beat, and my mood shot up, fizzing through my nerves, flaring high.

Declan scrawled his signature across the page, then pushed the papers away. Jason leaned down and his fingers turned the page around so it faced Portia. He looked at her. "Now you need to sign it as a witness."

She came over, picked up a pen from Declan's desk, and wrote her name and her details, then signed it too.

It was done, Saint was ours—Jason's son.

Jason glanced at me and I saw the look in his eyes that said he wanted to whoop with victory, but he held it in and looked back at Declan as he picked up the papers and slid them back into the envelope.

I wanted to start happy-dancing around the room.

Neither of us said anything as Jason turned and took my hand, but with his back to Declan he gave me a massive smile before he pulled me out of the office. Then we were both smiling.

"Portia, stay in here," Declan ordered behind us.

Justin was watching the office door when we walked out. He must have seen the outcome from our smiles. He smiled too.

Jason walked quickly when we crossed the office, a pace ahead of me, pulling me on, the grip on my hand tighter than it'd been before.

When we were out into the hall, he stopped and turned and his lips compressed, holding in a whoop, as his eyes widened.

I didn't hold mine in. "Ahhhhhhh!" I squealed with excitement, jumped at him and wrapped my arms around his neck.

He gripped me, lifting me off my feet. "Yay," he breathed into my ear.

We didn't go down in the elevator, we ran down the stairs, like kids, and then we ran out into the street. I stopped, opened my arms wide, and spun around, looking up at the sky. *Thank you.*

We went back to the hotel and faxed the signed documents to our lawyer so he could start finalizing everything. Then we went to the Bronx Zoo to celebrate.

Jason had taken me to the Bronx Zoo the day he'd proposed, then he'd taken me to Times Square and gotten down on one knee.

"One day we're gonna bring Saint here and we'll show him the Brooklyn Bridge Park and take him to Times Square, and then I'll say, Daddy proposed to me here."

Jason smiled at me as his hands embraced my cheeks, then he pulled my mouth to his. "I love you," he said over my lips just before he kissed me.

"Ahh!" I shouted, stepping away from him and laughing, as the sea lion in the pond beside us splashed the water up and over the side, soaking us.

"Saint would be laughing at that," Jason said as he wiped the water off his face.

CHAPTER SIXTEEN

Rachel

My fingers clasped the arms of the chair tightly.

"Rachel, it's true, you needn't always be on medication…" The psychologist smiled at me while his words pierced into my soul, a blade of hope. His elbows rested on his desk as I sat on the other side of it with Jason. "It's about understanding what triggers your most extreme swings and recognizing the signs when episodes begin, then balancing your medication while managing your lifestyle."

It sounded so simple, but I'd lived with bipolar for years— nothing about bipolar was simple. It was a complex, hideous monster that lived inside me.

"What I'd suggest you do, is go back to your psychologist in Portland and go on to a support plan. They can work with you intensely for six months or so. You'll need to see someone at least weekly, maybe twice-weekly. They'll monitor and review your medication and help you identify the risks and learn to spot the signs you need to be aware of, and look at what triggers episodes, and what steps to take when you feel episodes commencing and set a balance, and then perhaps you'll find in time that you'll only need medication at a point that episodes occur."

He sounded like he really believed my condition was manage-able. The hope inside flowered, but then I was at the higher end of my scale of moods. I'd have come in here and told the guy that I was fine, that everything was awesome and super-cool. But Jason had taken control of the conversation from the moment we'd gotten in and he'd stripped the facts bare. He'd told the guy everything from the point of view of an onlooker, not from the skewed perspective I had in my head. He'd brought me here, not just to get me some more help, but to get himself help.

The guy looked at Jason. "You'll make sure she goes."

He nodded.

If I'd been higher than I was I'd have probably taken this all really badly, but at my current level I could still understand that Jason needed help—and that I needed help—even when I was happy.

Jason had gripped my hand at various points through the discussion, as though he knew I could be hurt by it, the hold trying to tell me that it was not intended to hurt me.

"Well then, there's probably no more I can do for you here. But I'll send my report to you and to your psychologist in Portland."

"Thank you," Jason acknowledged.

Coming back to New York had given us Saint back, but it had given me Jason back too. I had hope in the future, a future that hadn't felt right when we'd left Oregon. He'd found the way to fix us, like he always did. I'd trust him more when we got home.

We stood up. I thanked the guy and shook his hand.

"Good luck, Rachel. Many people live well enough with bipolar, you mustn't let it frighten you. The trick is to learn to be the master of it, rather than let it be the master of you."

Prophetic words—but again, they were simple to say, but so difficult to do.

When we walked out of the office, Jason let go of my hand and wrapped an arm around me instead. "Shall we go back to the hotel and go for a last run in Prospect Park, then we'll hang out near Brooklyn Bridge if you want, and walk alongside the river, or go over to Manhattan?"

We were leaving early tomorrow; this was our last day here. My heart ached to be home with Saint, and it was going to be his first Thanksgiving soon.

"I'd like to go running, yeah, and then why don't we get a takeout and eat it in the Brooklyn Bridge Park, it can be our sort of anniversary dinner." It had been a year ago this week that we'd met. We hadn't celebrated it. "Then, after, can we go to Times Square and have coffee in the café where we drank after you proposed?"

He gave me a big wide smile and pulled me against him, to give me a squeeze. "I second all those ideas. We're going to be okay, you know that. There'll be another year to celebrate, and then another and before we know it, we'll be eighty."

I laughed. "I don't wanna be eighty."

The day was good, it brought back a hundred memories of when I'd fallen in love with him. We were friends again. He'd become like just a care-giver, looking out for me all the time. But today we ran and laughed together, and talked constantly.

My hand touched his cheek when we stood by the railing on the edge of the East River, in the Brooklyn Bridge Park. His looks knocked me in the chest with a sharp punch of acknowledgement, and for a moment I couldn't get the air into my lungs when I looked into his dark-brown eyes, framed by the dark lashes that had fascinated me from the first evening I'd met him. It was dusk, and in the dusk his features had a whole out-of-this-world magnificence. Love dug deep into my bones. I'd never loved anyone before him. I'd never love anyone but him and Saint—named for his saintly father, Jason.

"I love you." I'd said the words to him for the first time here, in the park, when he'd found out I was pregnant and the child wasn't his. He hadn't replied.

"I love you too, forever, no boundaries, Rach, and no restrictions, good and bad, in sickness and health."

"But it isn't sickness, is it? It's in madness and in health…"

"In madness and in health, then. I still want you. I still love you." He kissed my lips gently, and then properly, and our tongues danced around each other.

When he broke the kiss I rested my forehead on his shoulder and hung on to his leather jacket at his sides. I was always going to hang on to him, and love him. Always. I was keeping him and Saint.

CHAPTER SEVENTEEN

Rachel

I picked up the turkey. It was heavy.

"Do you want me to carry it?" Jason said. He was holding Saint—he'd hardly put Saint down since we'd come back, and he hadn't started back at the store yet. Although he'd caught up with the work on his online magazine.

"No, I wanna do it. Go and put Saint in his chair and sit down."

I couldn't believe how heavy the thing was, but it was important to me that it was me who presented it. This was my first family Thanksgiving.

The turkey looked good, all crispy and golden and it smelled amazing. I carried it into the dining room, a broad smile on my face. I was so proud that I'd cooked the bird, and I'd done loads of the rest of the dinner too, with Mom watching me and advising, but it was me who'd done the cooking.

I put it down on the table before Dad, so he could carve.

"This all looks lovely," Dad complimented.

"Thank you." Pride was the size of a mountain in me when I sat down. I'd proved to myself and the world I could cook a Thanksgiving dinner. It was another thing to tick off my I-can-be-a-good-mom list.

"Well, before we start let's shut our eyes and thank God for all this food."

146

"And I wanna be thankful for Jason and Saint, and you both," I added.

Mom reached over and held my hand. "We are all thankful that you are here with us too, Rachel."

I got up, hugged her, and gave her a kiss on the cheek. "Thank you for being such a wonderful mom." She laughed when I let her go. "And you'd better have a kiss too, Dad. I can't leave you out." I walked around the table, wrapped my arms around his neck, then kissed his cheek.

I couldn't leave my boys out either. I walked around and leaned down to kiss Jason. His head turned, so his lips pressed against mine. I let him go with a smile, then last of all, I kissed Saint's soft cheek, my hand running over his wispy hair.

I was a little high today, and they all knew it, my drugs hadn't quite brought me on to an even road yet, but I was enjoying myself and I didn't care what tomorrow brought. It was Thanksgiving, I was grateful for everything I had.

Dad carved and I helped dish up, and Saint, who was sitting in his new highchair between Jason and me, had his own little bowl. I cut up the turkey into teeny, tiny pieces and mixed it up with mashed vegetables. These were Saint's first proper solids, the only thing he'd had before was a little piece of white chocolate on Halloween. I'd wanted his first meal to be Thanksgiving.

Jason watched as I put a little on Saint's spoon and lifted it to his lips. "Open up."

"What are we going to use? Airplanes or choo choo trains?" Jason joked.

Saint's mouth opened, not because he knew there was food waiting, but in his usual speaking method of babbling sounds. I slipped the food in. It was like he tried to suck it, which pushed half of it out, while his eyes said, *what is this?* Jason laughed at Saint's expression.

I put another little bit into Saint's mouth. He looked at me and smiled as he sucked on it.

"He likes it. Doesn't he?" I looked at Mom.

She smiled.

"He sure does," Dad agreed.

"Don't forget to eat yours while it's hot, Rach." Jason nodded at my forgotten dinner.

I took a mouthful of turkey and trimmings, it was gorgeous, every bit of flavor tingled on my tongue. I'd never once eaten a Thanksgiving dinner, the only comparison I had to this was the silent, awkward Christmas lunch I'd eaten here when I'd first met Jason's parents.

I alternated then: a mouthful for me and a mouthful for Saint.

It was heaven, straight out of a fairytale and Prince Charming sat on the other side of Saint smiling at me.

When we'd finished the main course Jason stood to clear away the plates. "I'm giving Saint dessert," he said eagerly, staking his claim like it was a race to call it.

I laughed at him.

We had pumpkin pie, and Jason gave Saint a taste, watching him intently. Jason's eyes glowed with pride and pleasure.

This was my life. This was what I'd wanted my life to be. This would always be my vision of perfect. Whenever I became down I would think of this and try to recapture it.

When we'd finished eating Jason stood up and ran a hand over my hair. "You go sit down and give Saint a cuddle while he has his afternoon nap. The tradition in this house is that Dad and I do the dishes."

"Thanks."

Jason lifted Saint out of his highchair as I stood, then handed him to me. I stroked my little man's head and carried him over to the sofa, cradled him on one arm, and lay down beside him.

We looked each other in the eyes as I talked to him and sang to him until he fell asleep. I was glad to be back in Oregon—home.

"And if that horse and cart fall down, you'll still be the sweetest

148

little baby in town…" I brushed the hair off his forehead gently as his shallow breaths caressed my skin.

Jason walked into the room, clutching a large envelope in his hand. "It's here."

We'd been waiting for it, and expecting it for two days.

My lips pulled apart in a wide smile, breaking through the heavy hold my meds had on me.

He lifted a hand and cupped my face, looking into my eyes.

His eyes said *I love you*.

Then he looked down and opened the envelope.

"My heart's beating like mad," I said.

"So's mine," he answered.

"Wait a minute," Dad said. "Let's get a picture of the moment."

Jason looked up at him and laughed, it wasn't quite like me screaming in the labor room, or Jason cutting the cord, but Jason waited while Dad found his camera.

"Okay, now then, Son. Ready? Go!"

"Action," I breathed at Jason like we were cutting a film.

His eyes were wide and sparkly with tears when he pulled out the document. The court's stamp was on the front of it. "It's official," he said as he slid it right out of the envelope and held it up. "Saint's my son."

I hugged his waist. The joy inside me defied my meds. "We're a proper family."

"We always were. But now it's the law." His arm came down and wrapped around me, but he still clutched the paper. It brushed against my back.

When he let me go, he gritted his teeth and shut his eyes. A tear escaped from the corner of one of his eyes. He turned away trying to hide it and dropped the document on to a low table by the wall, then walked out of the room. I looked at Mom and Dad smiling like the Cheshire Cat from *Alice in Wonderland*. Then I followed Jason.

He was in our room, looking down at Saint, who was asleep. He leaned down and picked Saint up.

Saint's eyes opened and he smiled.

Jason lifted him up and held him in front of him, looking into Saint's eyes. "I've got you now and I'm keeping you forever." More tears, tears of love, filled Jason's eyes and caught in his dark eyelashes.

No matter how low I got, I wasn't ever going to doubt that he loved Saint and me, not anymore.

CHAPTER EIGHTEEN

Jason

"Hey, Jason! How are you?" The call rang across the community hall that my support group met in.

I looked over. "Hey." It was Roy, the guy who ran the group. He had a fifteen-year-old daughter with bipolar. He was always struggling to work out what was her being a typical teen and what was her bipolar.

I walked over.

Rachel had met all the people here and their families; we had social events, dinners and stuff, but once a month I drove over to these sessions on my own and spilled my guts out about how I felt. It had been hard to talk at first. Speaking to a bunch of strangers had felt weird. It wasn't like me. But I'd learned that I had to do it, because unless I shared this stuff, I'd crack up just as bad as Rach could.

The first time I hadn't said much, but because we all had one thing in common—loving someone with bipolar—they'd become friends by about my third session, and I learned from their problems as much as from what they had to say about my concerns.

"Roy," I said, to get his attention back when I got over to him. "I have news."

He turned around. "Sounds like good news too. What?"

"It's official, I have a son. I got the paperwork this week." Wow; the swell of emotion those words stirred. I hadn't thought it

151

would be any different, other than having a signature to wave at people. Saint had been christened Saint Macinlay, and he'd been born that. But… When I picked him up now I knew he was all mine, there was no risk of losing him. He was forever mine.

Roy's arms wrapped around me. Then when he let me go he shouted, "Hey, did you hear this, people? Saint is officially Jason's son! We have a new papa in the room!"

I was hugged over and over, and had my hand shaken.

These people had become like a second family to me. This was the room where I had permission to be weak once a month, and cry once a month, and say all the words I'd never admit I even thought to anyone else.

When I went home to Rach afterwards I was stronger. This place had become the foundation stone I was building the rest of my life on, and my life was steady, not on a fault line at all. I could see as far as old age with Rach. There was not one single doubt in my head that we could make it. We were good together— nope, we are—we are good together. The best.

AUTHOR NOTE

I wrote this story for everyone who read the first book *I Found You* and contacted me to ask for Jason and Rachel to have another book of their own. Thanks to everyone who loves these characters and for continuing to support them. But Jason and Rachel haven't entirely disappeared yet, you'll find them in some more of my contemporary stories.

To keep up with all my news why not follow me on Facebook? https://www.facebook.com/JaneLark.NABooks